The Key Players

Mesa Falls Ranch, Montana's premier luxury corporate retreat, got its start when a consortium bought the property.

The Owners

Weston Rivera, rancher

Miles Rivera, rancher

Gage Striker, investment banker

Desmond Pierce, casino resort owner

Alec Jacobsen, game developer

Jonah Norlander, technology company CEO

What do the owners have in common?

They all went to Dowdon School, where they were students of the late Alonzo Salazar.

The Salazars

Alonzo Salazar (dec.), retired teacher at Dowdon School, CEO of Salazar Media

Devon Salazar, copresident, Salazar Media, Alonzo's son

Marcus Salazar, copresident, Salazar Media, Alonzo's son, Devon's half brother

As these key players converge, dark secrets come to light in Big Sky Country...

Where family loyalties and passions collide...

"Have you had dinner?"

Desmond's gray eyes met hers, the invitation she saw in them tickling her insides in a way that felt all wrong for a man she needed to be wary around.

"I had something on the plane." It wasn't technically a lie because she'd eaten the protein bar she'd packed from home. "I can meet with any of your partners who are free this evening—"

"Me. I'm free this evening." He looked at her with a singular focus, like she was the only thing he had on his agenda for the rest of the week. Or—a wicked part of her brain amended—like she was the only item on his personal menu.

"Good." Nicole gave a nod of confirmation, hating that her voice had sounded breathless. Hungry. And *not* just because she'd eaten only a protein bar.

* * *

The Heir by Joanne Rock is part of the Dynasties: Mesa Falls series.

JOANNE ROCK

THE HEIR

HARLEQUIN

DESIRE

To my mom, for sharing her love of reading with me
so seamlessly. She still claims I learned to read on
my own before I went to school. Thank you, Mom.
I know you had a lot to do with that!

Recycling programs
for this product may
not exist in your area.

ISBN-13: 978-1-335-23271-7

The Heir

Copyright © 2021 by Joanne Rock

This edition published by arrangement with Harlequin Books S.A.

For questions and comments about the quality of this book,
please contact us at CustomerService@Harlequin.com.

Harlequin Enterprises ULC
22 Adelaide St. West, 40th Floor
Toronto, Ontario M5H 4E3, Canada
www.Harlequin.com

Printed in U.S.A.

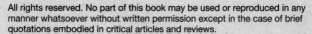

Dear Reader,

I can't believe we're at the end of the series already! I've loved exploring Mesa Falls and the friends who craved this retreat from the world, even if they didn't remember to visit as often as they should have. It was a good reminder to me that we all need to make time for friends and fun in our lives, no matter how busy we get.

I've been waiting for the mysterious character of Nicole to return to Mesa Falls. She had a brief appearance in *Rule Breaker*, but now she's back and she has some of the answers the men of Mesa Falls need. She is also the caretaker for her sister's orphaned child, and with everything at stake, she'll do anything to protect him. Even if that means going toe-to-toe with powerful and compelling Desmond Pierce to learn the identity of her nephew's father. But from Desmond's perspective, it's Nicole who has been keeping all the secrets. And if she really is ward to his dead friend's son, he will do everything in his power to keep her close. When these two start circling each other, sparks fly.

Join me for one last trip to western Montana for all the drama and sizzle of a Dynasties story!

Happy reading,

Joanne Rock

Joanne Rock credits her decision to write romance after a book she picked up during a flight delay engrossed her so thoroughly that she didn't mind at all when her flight was delayed two more times. Giving her readers the chance to escape into another world has motivated her to write over eighty books for a variety of Harlequin series.

Books by Joanne Rock

Harlequin Desire

Dynasties: Mesa Falls

The Rebel
The Rival
Rule Breaker
Heartbreaker
The Rancher
The Heir

Texas Cattleman's Club: Inheritance

Her Texas Renegade

Visit her Author Profile page at Harlequin.com, or joannerock.com, for more titles.

You can also find Joanne Rock on Facebook, along with other Harlequin Desire authors, at Facebook.com/harlequindesireauthors!

Prologue

Tired from a long night of travel, Nicole Cruz was still in bed when her phone rang on a Sunday morning.

She answered before fully awake, her thoughts still half in dreamland. She'd gotten a flight into San Francisco after midnight, but hadn't fallen into bed in San Jose until long afterward. It had been the first time she'd slept in her own home for nearly two weeks and she'd crashed hard.

"Hello?" Propping herself up on her elbow, she shoved tangled auburn hair from her eyes for a better peek at her phone screen when she realized two things at once.

First, this wasn't a normal phone call. She'd swiped the connect button on a video chat.

Second, her caller was Desmond Pierce, the rich and powerful casino resort owner who'd footed the bill for the return flight from Prince Edward Island yesterday so that Nicole and her nephew, Matthew, could answer his summons to western Montana. Nicole had insisted they stop in San Jose first so she could pick up a few of their things.

In reality, it was so she could surreptitiously drop Matthew off at his boarding school this morning. She hadn't told Desmond she had no intention of bringing the boy with her to Mesa Falls Ranch, the site of their appointed meeting later today to discuss the mystery of the teen's paternity.

"Good morning, Nicole." Desmond's deep voice resonated through the phone as his image filled her screen. His dark brown hair looked freshly cut around the sides, but the top was longer and slightly unruly. The bristle along his jaw was trimmed, too, but the shadow effect gave an edge to his tailored, European-cut suit.

Gray eyes zeroed in on her with startling clarity, making her all too aware of the skimpy pink camisole she'd slept in.

"Desmond," she said on an awkward gasp, dragging an oversize pillow in front of her to hide her breasts. "I—probably shouldn't have picked up."

Her pulse stuttered at the sight of him, his broad shoulders filling out his suit in an appealing way.

She'd liked the sound of his voice the first time they'd spoken on the phone earlier in the week. But seeing him now had the strangest effect on her, heightening her senses, making her very aware of him. And of herself and her lack of clothes. His gaze never left her face—at least not that she'd noticed. But she would swear there was a hint of amusement gleaming in their depths.

"Would you like to call me back when it's more convenient?" His tone remained even, as if unaware he was talking to a woman in bed. "I just wanted to give you the details for your flight today."

And you couldn't have just texted them? But she'd rather get the conversation over with now than have another talk hanging over her conscience, making her feel guilty about flying solo today.

"Now is fine," she assured him with false brightness, careful not to straighten up too much or she'd lose the pillow barrier she was banking on for coverage. "I should be up anyhow. I've got a lot to do before heading to the airfield."

"It's not too late for me to send a car for you," he offered, tapping the screen to life on a tablet as he spoke to her from behind a sleek mahogany desk. Behind him, a bank of windows overlooking the Bitterroot Mountains let her know he was already at Mesa Falls Ranch.

He hadn't been in residence during the few weeks she'd worked there. Shortly after Christmas she'd taken a job in guest services under an assumed name in the hope of learning more about the partners who ran the ranch. Before her sister's untimely death from a brain aneurysm last year, Lana had given Nicole reason to believe one of the men running Mesa Falls might be Matthew's father. But Nicole had been unceremoniously fired before she could learn the truth.

An event Desmond Pierce had since claimed hadn't been authorized by any of the partners. But at the time, her sudden termination had made her all the more wary of the men who owned Mesa Falls. She'd taken her nephew to Prince Edward Island in an effort to lie low and regroup, so it had rattled her to learn Desmond's private investigator had followed them. She'd spent days dodging the tail, finally giving in to talk to Desmond Pierce the third time the PI asked her to contact him. They'd spoken briefly on the phone two times before now. Yet until she learned more about his motives, she was planning to keep Mattie safely ensconced at his school. Besides, as a gifted child with autism spectrum disorder, her nephew sometimes struggled with change, and he'd been through more than enough these last months after losing his mom.

"I can get to the airport on my own," Nicole assured him, refusing to take more help than necessary. Bad enough he was sending his jet to pick her up today. "Am I still heading to Reid-Hillview?" she asked, naming the private airfield closest to her house.

"Yes," Desmond confirmed, rising to his feet and

buttoning his jacket with nimble fingers. Her focus lingered on his hand. "The pilot will be on-site at one o'clock to pick up you and Matthew, but he'll wait until you're ready, so don't rush."

Her stomach knotted. Guilt niggled for a moment before she shoved it aside. She refused to feel bad about doing what was best for Mattie. She would drop him off at school before heading to the airfield.

"I'll need a little longer than that." She dodged the mention of her traveling companion as she hugged the pillow to her chest and stood. "But I can probably be there by two."

"Excellent." Desmond rewarded her with a smile that had probably charmed far more worldly women than her. There was something compelling about him that went beyond good looks. "I appreciate you agreeing to see me."

He had an ease and competence that suggested he could accomplish anything. But then, wealth imbued people with that kind of confidence. He'd wanted Nicole and her nephew to come to Montana, so he'd had them followed until they caved to his terms.

Or so he thought. Nicole could at least keep him away from her nephew while Matthew was in school.

"It wasn't a decision I reached easily," she reminded him, needing this man to know she wasn't going to knuckle under to whatever demands he made once she was in Montana. "Being hounded by your detective didn't help your case if you really only wished to speak to me."

She feared that he and his friends—any one of whom might have fathered her nephew—would try to wrest guardianship of Matthew away from her. And he might as well know straight out of the gate that wasn't happening.

His jaw tightened at her rebuke, but he didn't deny it.

"Forgive me. I was unsure how else to right the wrong you were done while employed at the ranch. We'll make sure you're compensated for the abrupt termination."

She studied his features, looking for a hint as to his deeper motive, but his gray eyes revealed nothing. And while she was quickly running out of her personal reserves on her quest to find her nephew's father, she wouldn't be accepting financial gifts from a man who already wielded too much power.

"I'm not interested in that. I'm only coming to Montana to learn the truth about Mathew's connection to Mesa Falls."

Perhaps Desmond heard that it was a line in the sand for her, because he didn't argue. Then again, he didn't concede, either.

"I'm committed to helping you find the answers you're searching for." His gaze was unwavering.

Could she trust those words? Or was he more interested in making sure she didn't learn too much? It was impossible to tell. But she wouldn't let Desmond Pierce stop her in her quest.

And she damned well wouldn't allow his charismatic appeal to slip past her guard. Nothing was more important than protecting her nephew's best interests.

When she simply nodded, Desmond continued. "I look forward to seeing you when you land. There's a snowstorm rolling in later, so dress warm."

She knew it was for practical purposes that he was going to meet her personally, but a shiver still stole over her at the thought of stepping off the aircraft and coming face-to-face with this man for the first time.

Now the only man who'd seen her in bed in over a year.

Shaking off the wayward thought, Nicole wished her contact in Mesa Falls didn't have to be so damnably attractive.

"I'll see you soon. And…thank you." Disconnecting the call, Nicole made sure the screen went dark before she let go of the pillow.

She needed a shower to clear her head, and then she'd put her game face on for the day ahead. She would drop Matthew off at his school before boarding Desmond's private plane, then proceed to Montana alone to find out what the men of Mesa Falls had been hiding from her family. The next time she saw Desmond Pierce, he wasn't going to be happy with her.

One

Parking his SUV in a deserted lot behind the Ravalli County Airport in Hamilton, Montana, Desmond Pierce killed the engine. He'd tracked the flight of the light Gulfstream jet delivering his guests and timed his arrival carefully to meet Nicole Cruz and her ward for the first time.

Wind whipped off the jagged peaks of the Bitterroot range to the west, the snow-capped mountains casting long shadows on the valley as the sun dipped low in the sky. Desmond walked around to the front of the main hangar where the jet had just come to a full stop.

He, along with five friends, had purchased the plane at the same time they'd bought Mesa Falls

Ranch, where they'd invested heavily in sustainable ranching practices before expanding into a luxury resort to showcase their environmental initiatives. The ranch had been their memorial to a friend who'd died fourteen years ago when they'd been in boarding school together in Southern California. Until this winter, Desmond had thought he'd put that hellish time in his life behind him. But the old ghosts were back to plague him after a scandal hit Mesa Falls three months ago.

A scandal fueled to a boiling point thanks in part to his guests—a woman full of secrets, and her thirteen-year-old nephew, Matthew Cruz, whose unknown paternity was a new question mark in a past Desmond had tried hard to forget. But since the boy was linked to the owners of Mesa Falls, Desmond had stepped up to take the lead in dealing with Nicole.

It was his turn to be the face of the group, for one thing. For another? He'd experienced an unusual… *curiosity* about her during their conversations over the past week since his private investigator had located her.

Hell if he knew why he'd given in to the urge for a video call this morning. But images of her in that pink camisole had tormented him every minute since then.

He paused to stand under a metal awning sheltering one of the entrances into the hangar, waiting as the cabin door opened, a member of the ground crew securing the stairs. Tapping the snow off the toes of his boots, Desmond reviewed what he knew about Nicole from the detective's report. She'd taken a job at the ranch under an assumed name, using her time there to research the six partners who owned Mesa Falls. She believed one of them might be her nephew's father after the boy's mother died suddenly of an aneurysm. Before her death, Nicole's sister indicated that someone close to the ranch's owners had been financing Matthew's education. Nicole wanted to know why.

But Nicole had been fired by her supervisor, who quit immediately afterward. Nicole promptly grabbed Matthew from school and vanished, resulting in deeper mistrust between her and the men of Mesa Falls.

But Desmond needed her cooperation if they were going to figure out the boy's paternity. When he'd suggested she fly to Montana with her nephew for a meeting, she only agreed on the condition that he and his partners submit DNA samples for paternity tests—tests that had just come back negative for any matches. Results he had yet to share with Nicole, and which were going to give rise to a whole lot of new questions. He'd been afraid to give her too much of a heads-up on the news for fear she'd change her mind about returning to Montana.

Now shadows stirred near the cabin door, making Desmond straighten where he stood. He'd seen photos of the boy, so he knew generally what to expect. Matthew—with his sandy hair, lean frame and dark brown eyes—bore little resemblance to anyone Desmond knew.

Nicole had thick auburn waves and eyes the same deep brown as her nephew's, with features Desmond had memorized even before their video call. The detective had given him a still photo pulled from the ranch's security footage during the weeks she'd been an employee. At that time, Weston Rivera had been in charge of Mesa Falls while Desmond had been embroiled in running his casino resort on the northern shore of Lake Tahoe, so his path had never crossed Nicole's.

A missed opportunity? Or was it just as well considering the interest she stirred in him that didn't have anything to do with her connection to Mesa Falls? He didn't know what spurred the reaction. She was lovely, certainly. But that alone had never been enough to spark the kind of awareness he had for this woman. The casino he ran attracted wealth and beauty in direct proportion to one another. Nicole had something different. Warmth. Fire. He'd heard it in her voice when they spoke on the phone. Seen it in her eyes in that video call.

He'd been hungry to meet her from their first conversation, eager to see if that would ease the craving he had for more of her. Maybe that had been part of the reason he'd video-called this morning. Perhaps he hoped the fascination with her might ease once

he saw her, but if anything, he was even more preoccupied with thoughts of her.

Now, the shadows around the cabin door shifted
and she stood just thirty yards from him, poised at
the top of the stairs. Dressed in a fawn-colored coat
with knee-high black leather boots, she reached one
gloved hand to steady herself on the handrail while
she used the other to restrain the mass of red curls
from the tug of the cold winds.

If any part of him had hoped the magnetic effect
she had on him would dissipate once he saw her in
person, the hope evaporated now. In the eight years
he'd spent building his business, it hadn't been difficult for Desmond to keep relationships simple and
straightforward. He'd invested everything he had
in building the casino business from nothing. He'd
devoted little time to women, and then only in the
most cursory way. But right now, even with the wind
chill hovering at freezing, he felt sparks just looking at Nicole Cruz.

As if called by his thoughts, she glanced toward
the hangar suddenly, her gaze finding him. It was
damned fanciful of him to think she might feel the
same pull between them, so he straightened and
headed toward the tarmac to meet her.

He was halfway to the metal stairs when it occurred to him there was no one else with Nicole.
The pilot was already on the pavement, exchang-
ing a few words with the guy from the ground crew
while the two of them looked over the aircraft.

Nicole's bag was on the small carpet at the base of the fold-down steps.

Bag. Singular.

Suspicion stirred as his gaze darted back to hers, but he held himself in check while he greeted her.

"Welcome, Nicole." He extended a hand when he halted a few feet from her. "Thank you for making the trip."

His fingers closed around the leather of her gloved palm, and he had a brief impression of her warmth. She was tall for a woman, her brown eyes nearly level with his in her heeled boots.

"Thank you for having me. I'm as eager as you are to find answers about my nephew," she assured him before she pulled back, her tone cool as they sized one another up under the harsh glare of the outdoor lights. Her face appeared free of cosmetics, yet her full lips were a rich berry color that drew his attention as she spoke.

For a moment, his attention snagged on her word choice. But of course, he wouldn't be *having* her. She was here in the interests of her ward, and Desmond was here to protect the men who were like brothers to him. It wouldn't be possible to explore an attraction to her, even if it was distracting as hell.

A red curl escaped her grasp and wavered along her cheek. Behind her, the worker from the ground crew closed the cabin door while another woman jogged toward the runway and pulled on a headset, lights under one arm to direct air traffic.

"Speaking of your nephew." Desmond glanced from Nicole to the jet and then back again, wondering what kind of game she was playing. "Where is Matthew?"

They all wanted to meet the boy, whom their former mentor, Alonzo Salazar, had secretly supported. Once they met Matthew, maybe they would recognize the connection. See something familiar in the boy's features or manner that they couldn't pick up through a mere photo.

Her pointed chin jutted at the question.

"Back in boarding school." She reached for the handle of her rolling canvas bag as if that handful of words could end the discussion—the same one they'd had over the phone when he'd first arranged for her to bring the boy to Montana.

Annoyance flared. Desmond took the suitcase for her, his hand brushing hers as the sound of an approaching aircraft hummed on the breeze.

"We had an agreement," he reminded her tightly, unaccustomed to his directives not being followed. At his casino, he ran a smooth, efficient business because his plans were executed to the letter. Even at Mesa Falls, where he shared control with his partners, there was still discussion, compromise and agreement.

Not open defiance.

Her full lips compressed into a flat line before she spoke. "As I recall, we had a *dis*agreement since I wasn't keen on being followed by your private detective. I told you Matthew didn't do well with change, and that he needed to return to a known environment where he thrives. You insisted I bring him against my better judgment."

The wind kicked up around them. The pilot for Desmond's jet returned to the cockpit as if to park the aircraft for the night.

"Those were the terms," Desmond reminded Nicole.

"Your terms, not mine." Her brown eyes flashed with a fire that didn't come through her cool words, revealing a passion that might have intrigued him if she hadn't just upended all his plans. "Now, I'm here and I'm going to find answers with you or without you. So what will it be, Desmond? Do you want me to return to Mesa Falls with you or not?"

A few minutes later, Nicole sat in the passenger seat of Desmond Pierce's shiny black luxury SUV, her suitcase stowed in the back as he drove west toward the Bitterroot mountain range and Mesa Falls Ranch.

It was clear from the long silence following his terse request that she accompany him, Desmond was not pleased with her refusal to dance to his tune.

Too. Bad.

She focused on the scenery outside the window as they drove closer to the jagged peaks, the open fields dotted with the occasional barn or equipment shed. She was done caring what the privileged men of Mesa Falls thought about her, so Desmond could brood all he wished. Her sole concern was finding her nephew's father and holding him financially accountable for contributing to his son's upbringing. Even though his education was taken care of by Salazar's book profits, it was an arrangement she wasn't completely comfortable with. Mattie had a unique set of skills and needs that were well met at the private school where he'd boarded the last few years before Nicole's sister, Lana, had died suddenly. The hurt of Lana's passing still caught Nicole off guard sometimes, stopping her short in the middle of the day, the pain of it so sharp she felt like she couldn't breathe.

But remembering Mattie helped. Especially when she knew that her sister's son would naturally grieve even more for Lana than she did. The fact that Lana had died without revealing anything of Mattie's father—other than a vague reference to the child being taken care of thanks to Alonzo Salazar's tell-all book—complicated Nicole's life exponentially. She hadn't minded taking time away from her freelance graphic design job to search for answers, but the weeks had stretched to months and her savings dwindled. She didn't have the luxury of turning down Desmond Pierce's offer of making the travel arrangements for her return to Montana.

But she couldn't ignore her nephew's needs in favor of the man currently in the driver's seat. Turning her attention back to him, Nicole let her gaze wander over Desmond while he drove. Even angry with her, he remained ridiculously attractive. Thoughts of their morning phone call—waking up to his face while she was still in bed—had never been far from her mind today.

And Desmond wasn't just pleasing to the eye with his stormy gray eyes, dark hair and shadowed jaw that called a woman's fingers to test the texture of the bristles there. There was more to it than a strong build and fine physique evident even under the winter layers of his black wool jacket with a taupe-colored fisherman's sweater underneath. It was something intangible about the way he looked at her, the way he spoke, the way he moved that just flipped a switch inside her.

A strange phenomenon she'd never experienced before. In the past, the few men who'd been in her life had been there for practicality's sake—someone fixed her up with a friend because it was easier to group date. But the sexy, charged encounters that other women seemed to have just didn't happen for her.

Although one look at Desmond—one moment to feel the draw between them—gave her some clue about what she'd been missing. It seemed wholly unfair that the universe put this compelling man in her path right *now* when she needed to focus on finding her nephew's father. Barely containing her frustrated sigh, Nicole couldn't stand another moment of the heavy silence in the luxury SUV. The wealth of supple leather and sleek engineering in the vehicle did little to put her at ease, the bespoke interior reminding her how much power and influence this man wielded.

"I'm not sure we're going to find the answers we seek about Matthew's dad if we aren't speaking," she observed, unbuttoning her long coat now that she was out of the damp cold.

Or maybe she just needed to cool down the heat of her thoughts.

Desmond's fingers flexed on the steering wheel as the sun dipped out of sight behind the snowcapped mountains, leaving the sky painted with streaks of purple tinged with gold.

"We'll come up with a new plan." His glance slid sideways. "We have no choice."

The undertone of blame nettled.

"I hope you're not expecting me to feel guilty about doing what's best for Matthew." She'd expected better from Desmond based on the two phone calls she'd had with him. He'd eased her concerns about returning to Montana, and—she'd thought—done what he could to make the trip easier. "I won't apologize for taking care of him to the best of my ability. I owe my sister that much."

She was horrified to hear the crack in her voice as the last words left her mouth. She would not show weakness now. Except thoughts of never seeing Lana again still had the power to take her legs right out from under her.

Blinking fast, she glanced out the window again

as the darkness deepened. Near the road, a tractor tilled the ground with the help of headlights.

If Desmond heard the emotions in her voice, he didn't acknowledge them. But he continued, more gently, "What's Matthew like?"

"Brilliant," she said without hesitation, grateful for the conversational about-face. "The more time I spend with him, the more I admire my sister for recognizing his unique abilities early on and finding a program to help him thrive. He's great in math, with an uncanny memory for facts. He also draws really well, which has given us some common ground, since I work in graphic design."

She'd been fascinated by her nephew's detailed ink sketches of skyscrapers and cityscapes he drew while in Prince Edward Island. The last-minute trip had been an attempt to keep him out of the spotlight in case the news of how he'd benefited from the Salazar book became public, but Desmond had assured her that information—for now—remained private.

He steered off the county route and onto a private road, the movement hitching at his coat sleeve enough to expose a sleek silver Patek Philippe watch that cost more than she made in a year.

"How are you adjusting to life as the guardian of a thirteen-year-old boy?" he asked with surprising insight. Caring, even.

"Honestly?" She thought about how much her life had changed in the months since her sister died. Her world had been flipped on its ear. "It's been a little overwhelming."

"I think any parent of a thirteen-year-old would agree it's a lot of work." He gave a nod to the operator of a tractor with a snowplow attachment traveling in the opposite direction.

"It's not because of Mattie, though," she assured him, unwilling to give a false impression of her smart sweetheart of a nephew. "He's great. I just worry I'm not doing things the right way. I'll wake up at night in a panic that I messed up his health insurance or somehow compromised the educational services he receives any time I go into the school's website to file a form."

Desmond's phone chimed through the dashboard Bluetooth, but he hit a button to silence the screen, giving her his undivided attention.

"From what I hear, that's effective parenting. If you're worried whether or not you're doing a good job, you probably are."

For a moment, she thought his tone sounded almost wistful. But one glance over at his inscrutable expression told her she must be imagining it. Everything about Desmond Pierce suggested he'd been born to wealth and privilege, a background underscored by his attendance at the exclusive Dowdon School on the West Coast. All of the Mesa Falls owners had attended the expensive private institution that educated so many of America's elite.

"I hope that's true." She kept an eye on the road

ahead for her first glimpse of the ranch after weeks away from Montana. "Has there been any progress from your private investigator about who was responsible for terminating me during my brief time working here?"

A muscle flicked in Desmond's jaw, a brief sign of displeasure despite his impassive visage.

"Yes. And I can assure you it wasn't any of my partners. But I'd like to save the debriefing until after you're settled." He glanced her way, his expression thoughtful. "I realize trust won't come easily for either of us, but I want answers about your nephew as much as you do."

The sincerity in his voice was hard to miss. From their phone calls arranging this meeting, she'd had a glimpse of how much Desmond trusted his business partners. She understood he wanted to clear their names of all scandal having to do with the book their mentor had written that profited off real people's misfortunes. But she didn't share his faith in the men of Mesa Falls. Someone powerful had made sure she lost her job here.

And maybe there was a reason Lana hadn't identified the father of her child. Maybe he wasn't a good person.

"That's fine," she agreed as the impressive main lodge came into view. Built in the style of the National Parks lodges, the split-log structure combined woodsy appeal with elegance, the landscape lighting drawing attention to deep second-story balconies and huge glass windows overlooking the Bitterroot River. "But keep in mind I'm not some kind of diva guest who needs to unpack twelve suitcases' worth of clothes for every occasion. I'll be ready to go in an hour at most."

Desmond was silent for a moment as he pulled the SUV around the horseshoe driveway, stopping under a sheltered portico in front of the lodge. A liveried attendant approached the vehicle, but Desmond halted him with a gesture.

"Would you like to have an early dinner?" Desmond turned toward her, his thigh shifting against the leather seat now that the vehicle was parked.

His gray eyes met hers, the invitation she saw in them tickling her insides in a way that felt all wrong for a man she needed to be wary around. If any one of the Mesa Falls partners turned out to be Mattie's father—Desmond included—they would have cause to take the boy away from her. Certainly any one of them would have the financial ability to hire the best attorneys to make that happen. Her stomach knotted.

"I had something on the plane." It wasn't technically a lie, because she'd eaten the protein bar she'd packed from home. She had questions she wanted answered about her sister, and the sooner she got started on the quest, the sooner she could leave Montana for good. "I can meet with any of your partners who are free this evening—"

"Me. I'm free this evening." He looked at her with a singular focus, like she was the only thing he had on his agenda for the rest of the week. Or—a wicked part of her brain amended—like she was the only item on his personal menu. "I'll meet you in the lobby in an hour, and we'll get started."

Her pulse kicked up in answer, as if he'd suggested something more intimate than a business meeting. Her reactions were all off around him, distracting her from something important. She needed to put her nephew first no matter how confusing the sensual undercurrent between her and her host.

"Good." She gave a nod of confirmation, hating that her voice had sounded breathless. Hungry. And *not* just because she'd only eaten a protein bar. Grinding her teeth against the surge of unfamiliar feelings, Nicole shoved them to the back of her mind. "See you then."

She must have missed a sign between Desmond and the valet, because no sooner were the words out of her mouth than the passenger side door was opened by an attendant.

"Welcome to Mesa Falls, miss," the young man said with a smile while another plucked her suitcase from the back. "I hope you enjoy your stay."

Off-balance but unwilling to show it, Nicole wrapped her coat tighter around her waist and turned to step outside.

But not before Desmond's parting words to her stroked along her senses.

"I'm looking forward to it, Nicole."

Two

Thoughts full of Nicole Cruz, Desmond walked into the state-of-the-art stables near the paddock, the building that housed the ranch offices. While not as outwardly showy as his private office at his casino resort in Tahoe, the Mesa Falls executive suite complemented the place.

The stables downstairs were immaculately kept, for one thing, with each horse's name on a stall. Only the best of their stock was kept here, prized studs available for a fee. He paused in front of a heavy stall door to stroke the nose of a racing champion quarter horse, Sundancer, his personal favorite. The chestnut tossed his proud head and whinnied when Desmond headed for the stairs to the upper story.

The commitment to horses was an important mission of a ranch run in memory of Zach Eldridge, a schoolmate of the owners who'd cliff-jumped to his death on a horseback riding trip fourteen years ago. The friends who'd been with Zach that weekend had bought the ranch together as a way to keep his memory alive, although they'd never agreed on the exact circumstances of his death. The conditions had been all wrong for the jump. Had Zach known he wouldn't survive and jumped to end his life? The question haunted them still. Zach had been the closest friend Desmond ever had, even though their friendship had been far too brief.

It was always tough to be in Mesa Falls because of the memories it evoked of Zach, even though his dead friend had never visited Montana. Just being in a place that Zach's friends purchased to honor him messed with Desmond's head. And now, chances were good that Matthew Cruz could be Zach's son, which meant Desmond needed to find a way to get comfortable with talking about Zach, as Nicole would obviously have a lot of questions. Starting with—how could they prove Zach was the father?

Desmond huffed out a frustrated breath as he reached the top of the staircase. Since he needed to pick up Nicole again in an hour, there was no point making the longer trip to his house on the ranch property when the executive suite had been built close to the main lodge.

He shoved open the exterior door, giving a nod to

the administrator in the seat out front as he passed him, grateful the assistant appeared busy with a phone call, so Desmond didn't have to make small talk. He unlocked the private office in back and allowed the door to close behind him before sinking into the high-backed leather chair behind the glass-topped stainless-steel desk. He swiveled to look out the windows at the mountains and expelled a long breath.

Nicole had completely disregarded his request to bring her nephew to the ranch. What's more, she made no apology for doing what she thought was best for Matthew.

I just worry I'm not doing things the right way.

Her words about parenting echoed in his mind, reminding him that she was her ward's advocate first and foremost, no matter what Desmond wanted. It inconvenienced him. But at the same time, the part of him that had been emotionally abandoned by his own parents cheered for her fierce dedication to the boy. What child wouldn't want her on his side?

The thought wreaked havoc with his plan to interrogate her about her sister's past, and it sure as hell didn't sit well with his fear that Zach would turn out to be Matthew's father. The idea of his best friend's son growing up without a father thrust another knife of guilt into a conscience already weighed down with ways he'd failed Zach.

Underneath those concerns lurked a whole lot of undeniable physical attraction. Too often he'd found his thoughts drifting to the video call that had given him a glimpse of the too-sheer pink camisole. Meeting her in person had done nothing to dim that memory or the damnable interest that went with it.

The chime of the intercom halted the feature film of tantalizing images replaying through his head.

He cursed the interruption even as he knew he should welcome it, then pressed the button to answer. "Yes?"

"Miles Rivera to see you," the assistant intoned through the speaker.

Miles had returned from the West Coast already? His friend and fellow partner in the ranch must have something important on his mind if he'd left Los Angeles where he was supposed to be reuniting with his social media star sweetheart, Chiara Campagna.

"Send him in," Desmond returned, getting to his feet as the office door opened to admit Miles Rivera.

The older of the two Rivera brothers who'd attended school with him, Miles was a levelheaded rancher in contrast to his wilder, risk-taking sibling, Weston.

Desmond came around to the front of the desk to shake hands with his friend.

"Good to see you, Miles." He gestured to one of the leather armchairs near a window overlooking the paddock. "Do you have time to take a seat?"

"Definitely," he answered in his distinctive, slightly raspy voice. Miles unbuttoned his dark blue jacket before he sat, his clothing game always top-notch. "Chiara and I flew back this morning after deciding to spend a couple of weeks in Mesa Falls to reconnect. She enjoyed the privacy of life in Montana."

His smile was unmistakable. And the obvious happiness on his face was something Desmond hadn't seen in the serious rancher for a long time.

"I'm glad things worked out for you two," Desmond observed, knowing how desperate Miles had been to see her and put things right between them.

"I'm grateful as hell for the second chance. But I was curious to hear your initial thoughts on our guest while Chiara is having a meeting this morning. Do you think Nicole is here to make trouble?"

Defensiveness spiked as Desmond took the seat by his prep school buddy, but that made no sense when they all had every reason to be on guard around Matthew Cruz's guardian.

"Hard to say. We didn't speak for long on the drive from the airport, but I'm seeing her again shortly. She's eager for answers."

"Aren't we all?" Miles asked dryly, reaching toward the windowsill to flip a decorative hourglass full of dark sand. At one time, they'd used the device as a silent timer for group meetings when they were setting up the ranch business. "Did you see our alma mater is cashing in on Alonzo Salazar's name now that our former teacher has been unmasked as the author of *Hollywood Newlyweds*?"

"What's this?" He'd been too busy with the logistics of getting Nicole and Matthew to Montana to notice much else.

"The Dowdon School is hosting their fiftieth anniversary party this year as a fundraiser—"

"I remember. We're all attending." Desmond had RSVP'd a week ago.

"—and they've started running social media teasers about famous alumni, including a pitch about Salazar's book. Something like, 'At Dowdon, you'll be in the know.'" Miles quoted the ad copy with a heavy dose of mockery.

Desmond scrubbed a hand over his head. "How could they think that's a good idea? That book ruined lives."

"Some media relations expert probably convinced them there's no such thing as bad press." Miles sat forward in his seat. "But I spoke with a rep at the school today to let them know my thoughts on that, and when I did, I also talked them into renting out our old dorm rooms for us that weekend."

Desmond's gut dropped as memories slammed him. "You can't seriously want to stay there?" They were small, for one thing, especially since most of them would be attending with significant others. But for another, the whole trip was going to remind him of Zach.

The small room he'd once shared with him most of all.

"I get it." Miles leaned forward in his chair to clap a consoling hand on Desmond's shoulder. "I do. But this gala might be a chance to really close the doors on that time. For good. Besides, we don't have to sleep there. I just figured we could have a pre-party toast on-site before we head to the gala."

"Right. Okay." He nodded, recognizing it was probably a good plan even if it stirred old ghosts for him personally.

"Good. Glad you're on board." Miles rose to his feet again, a rare smile pulling one corner of his mouth. "Well, I told Chiara I'd meet her, so I'd better be on my way. Chiara is organizing a dinner for Nicole and Matthew, by the way, so we can meet the boy."

Desmond walked with him to the door. "About that—"

"I don't envy you entertaining a thirteen-year-old." Miles mused as he withdrew his cell phone from his jacket pocket. "Weston and I were hellions at that age."

Irritation stabbed through him again. "Nicole didn't bring the boy with her."

Miles stopped short, his phone forgotten. "But that was part of the deal. Seeing him in person might let us see a familiar gesture or some other small detail that we might miss in a photo."

The defensiveness he'd felt about Nicole earlier in the conversation redoubled. And what was that about? He'd had the same problem with her decision that Miles did now. But he couldn't deny her reasoning had gotten to him.

"She's protecting him." He recalled her expression when she'd told him *I'm not some kind of diva guest*... "She's not what I expected."

Frowning, Miles narrowed his gaze. "Let's just hope she keeps away from the media. I don't think we want any more attention on Alonzo Salazar or that damned book of his."

Desmond agreed. News that the profits from their mentor's book supported a fatherless child would be sensation enough. But if the father proved to be Zach—a man whose death had been kept quiet for years—the outcry would be significant. Who would support the green initiatives of the ranch if the owners had been part of the reason that a child with special needs had grown up without knowing about his father?

"That won't happen on my watch." No matter how much Nicole infiltrated his thoughts, Desmond would protect Mesa Falls and the legacy they'd built for Zach. "I'll ask Nicole about a dinner tomorrow if you still want to meet with her."

After agreeing to message him in the morning, Miles left, and at the same time Desmond's phone buzzed with a notification.

Couldn't sit still in the lobby. Meet at the dartboard in great room instead.

Desmond didn't need to check the identity of the texter. Nicole hadn't been kidding that she hadn't required much time to settle into her room—only forty-five minutes had passed since they'd parted ways.

Pocketing his phone, he locked up behind him and headed to meet her.

Closing one eye, Nicole focused on the bull's-eye while an old country classic played on the sound system in the lodge's great room. The tile floor under her feet was softened with colorful Aztec rugs in the conversation areas of the room, the reds and burnt oranges repeated in the throw pillows and framed prints on the natural log walls. A small bar held top-shelf liquors under the watchful eye of a stuffed American bison standing near the pool table. Bar stools were padded in black-and-white cowhide.

A couple of older women sat at a nearby table, their conversation punctuated with occasional laughter. Other than the two of them and a twentysomething male bartender engrossed in his phone, Nicole had the room to herself. The whole gaming area was empty except for her. The pool table was untouched, the balls racked in the center of the green felt. A classic Skee-Ball arcade game waited for her to try next.

For now, in front of the dartboard, Nicole lined up her shot in an attempt to burn off nervous energy. She spun the tungsten barrel a few times in her fingers, getting used to the dimpled grip. She preferred razor cuts or crosshatching, but the darts were high quality, unlike the sets she'd come across in most pubs that were brass with warping or split tips. Flexing her wrist, she fired.

One. Two. Three.

A low whistle sounded behind her, alerting her to a newcomer.

Turning, she spotted Desmond's gray gaze focused on the board where her darts had notched in a tight group.

"Three triple twenties." He arched a brow before his attention veered toward her. "Impressive."

She doubted she had many skills that would impress this cosmopolitan man, but her father had taught her his favorite game well. "Do you play?"

"No." He edged around the pool table until he leaned a shoulder against the Skee-Ball game, where he could observe her more closely. "As the owner of a casino, I've learned to avoid games people bet on."

"Wise of you, I'm sure." She could only imagine how many people lost hefty sums under this man's watch. "But darts isn't a game of chance. The outcome rewards skill."

"Poker does, too. Sometimes those games are almost more dangerous, because players can have false ideas about their skill level." His gaze lifted to the board again. "Although there's no denying you've got a good throw."

"We can play just for fun then." She reached for the green darts in a game box on a low table nearby, then passed three to him, settling them in his hand.

The look in his eyes gave her pause, his pupils

dilated so only a ring of pale silver remained on the outside. Her finger remained on the heel of his palm before she yanked it back.

"What?" she asked, suddenly too aware of him. Of herself.

Her heart skipped a beat and then sped too quickly. Her skin heated.

"I'm tempted to play with you, Nicole." He lowered his head to speak more softly. "But I think we should talk first."

She swallowed, her mouth dry. Her thoughts scrambled. Was it possible he experienced the attraction to the same degree she did? Could he be struggling hard against it, too?

"Right. That's why I'm here." She'd taken up the game because she felt antsy and anxious to begin her quest for answers. But now? She felt even more antsy and anxious, for a whole other host of reasons. Warmth crawled over her skin.

"We can speak in my office," he offered, returning the darts to the metal game box with the others. "Or find a quiet table in the back."

The idea of being alone with him sizzled through her already overheated senses. She couldn't afford to let this heady awareness sidetrack her.

"Let's go watch the ice-skaters." She blurted the first outdoor alternative that occurred to her. Having worked at the ranch, she knew the terrain well, and right now, cold air and more space would be welcome. "That is, it should be a nice night by the pond. I saw a bonfire burning out the window earlier."

"Did you bring a jacket?" Glancing around, he spotted the coat she'd worn earlier and retrieved it from where she'd thrown it over the back of a chair. "The temperature has dropped since I picked you up at the airport. Are you sure you want to go out?"

Seeing his broad hands splayed on her coat spurred more thoughts about his touch, which was all the incentive she needed. "I'd love some fresh air."

She reached to take the garment, but he shifted behind her to lay it gently on her shoulders. A shiver stole through her, and she hoped he didn't notice.

"What about you?" Stepping away from him quickly, she took in his black dress shirt, dark jeans and boots.

"I left it with Simon up front." He referenced one of her former colleagues in guest services. "I'll grab it on our way out."

Minutes later, they circled around the building on a stone path, through a courtyard behind the lodge and toward the skating pond. Drifts of snow still circled the pond, but the ice had been cleared along with the pathways, the property impeccably groomed by the grounds staff.

"Are you warm enough?" Desmond asked as they reached a wooden bench close enough to see the ice but isolated enough for a private conversation.

He gestured for her to sit.

"I'm good," she answered honestly, grateful for

the chilly night air cooling her cheeks. Even the added layers of winter coats between their bodies was welcome. She took a seat on the bench and enjoyed the sounds of the skate blades on the ice mingling with laughter and the low hum of conversation from around the bonfire on the opposite side of the small pond.

"How does it feel to be back?" He seated himself beside her, not too close, but then again, having him within five feet of her stirred her insides. "I hope there's no awkwardness for you."

His thoughtful concern caught her off guard. Her gaze skittered away from him to focus on the skaters. "Not really. I wasn't employed here long enough to make friends, so I don't think anyone spent time wondering what happened to me when I was terminated."

She followed the progress of a young father holding a little girl's hand as she wobbled on her skates. She was probably four or five years old, mittens hanging from strings from her coat sleeves while she clutched her dad's hand in both of hers, giggling as he towed her along on her skates.

When Desmond was silent for a long moment, she turned to him again and found him studying her. He'd stretched his arm along the back of the bench behind her while she'd been absorbed in the skating, and she swore she could feel the warmth of his hand on her back even though he didn't touch her.

"You were here for almost a month," he said slowly. "I'm sure people noticed your absence."

"I'm a bit of a loner," she found herself saying, realizing too late she was disclosing something personal. Something he didn't need to know about her. She straightened more, putting distance between his hand and her back. "You mentioned earlier that you had learned more about who'd fired me?"

"Our private investigator looked into it. Your supervisor turned in his notice the next day, and he wasn't easy to track down, but apparently he'd been given orders from Vivian Fraser."

"I don't recognize that name."

"She was Alec Jacobsen's assistant until last week, when she was arrested." She knew Alex Jacobsen was one of his partners, a game designer. "At the time, your supervisor assumed the order to fire you came from Alec."

His words about an arrest shocked her. A chill went through her at the thought of someone criminal so close to her. Or worse—close to Mattie.

"Why was she arrested?" Unthinking, she reached toward Desmond, her hand landing on his knee. "Could Matthew be in danger?"

"No." Desmond's hand covered hers. Steady. Calming. "She's still behind bars. And her arrest was for harassing Chiara Campagna—"

"The social media star." Puzzling over the details now that her panic about her nephew had eased, she would have freed her fingers, but Desmond's palm still covered them. "I did notice she posted a couple of photos from Mesa Falls recently."

"Yes." He nodded, but the word was clipped, and she had the feeling there was more to that story. "Vivian apparently has feelings for Alec, and she thought she was protecting his privacy by threatening Chiara if she continued to post about Mesa Falls."

She tipped her head back to peer up at the stars, struggling to pull the pieces together. What was she missing? Sliding her fingers free of Desmond's, she folded them in her lap, still feeling his touch where it had been moments before. Every whorl of his fingertips left an impression that hummed along her skin.

"Why do you think she had me fired? Do you think she saw me as a threat, as well?" Recalling her time spent here, trying to find out more about Alonzo Salazar and the identity of Matthew's father, Nicole remembered there was only one person who knew her real goal. "Only April Stephens, the financial investigator who looked into Salazar's book, knew what I was doing."

"But April shared your motives with Weston Rivera, who revealed it to the other owners." His breath huffed a mist of white between them before it cleared, the night air feeling suddenly too cold.

Although maybe the loss of Desmond's touch had more to do with the chill.

"So all of you knew what I was doing here. And you think Vivian found out because she worked closely with Alec?" She had her work cut out for her here with too many questions that still needed answers in order to offer her nephew security. Stability. He was a defenseless kid who needed her.

"That's the theory." Desmond's gray gaze missed nothing as it wandered over her. "We should go in soon. You'll catch a chill."

His other palm slid from the back of the bench to rest between her shoulder blades. The contact should have just warmed her, perhaps. But even through her coat, the touch reminded her of the fierce attraction that lingered between them.

Or, for her, at least.

Did he feel it?

"I still have so many questions, but I'm out of my depth with all of this," she admitted, referring to the intrigue that hung heavy over the ranch even though it aptly applied to the magnetic pull she felt toward the man beside her. "Now I feel like I need to speak to Chiara Campagna, if that's possible."

"She's organizing a dinner with the other partners, so we can all talk then." His hand rubbed the center of her back gently. "Let's go in, Nicole. You must be exhausted after the flight last night and another one today."

"And I woke up early—" She cut herself off, remembering the nature of the call that awoke her.

Seeing Desmond on her phone. Feeling her senses wake up along with the rest of her. What possessed her to bring that up?

She could tell he was remembering that moment,

as well. His gaze darkened. But he rose to his feet and tugged her after him. "Since that was my fault, I feel all the more compelled to send you inside. You can get some sleep, and I'll text you tomorrow with details about the dinner so you can meet Chiara and the other partners."

She nodded mutely, not trusting her wayward mouth not to betray her in more ways.

Walking beside Desmond, Nicole returned to the lodge at his side, her thoughts still on his dictate that she get some sleep. She'd awoken in bed this morning to the sight of this man, albeit on her screen. And she knew without question she'd return to bed tonight with the image of him on the backs of her eyelids.

Three

Late the next morning, Desmond had the ranch's rifle range all to himself. The mountain meadow had a covered stand to protect guests from inclement weather where they could practice shooting reactive targets up to four hundred yards away. But for Desmond, shooting wasn't about getting out of the elements. Instead, he lay prone on a short rise off to one side of the covered stand, where a ranch employee waited to take his weapon when he finished.

His steel targets were just over a thousand yards away, the sport made more challenging by the crosswind coming off the mountain. He'd been lying here for almost an hour, getting a feel for the steady wind versus the gusts, timing his shots when the latter went still.

He'd hoped to clear his head after a restless night without much sleep, his thoughts too full of Nicole Cruz. So far it wasn't working. He still wanted her with a hunger he'd never felt for any woman, and telling himself she was off-limits wasn't making a dent in that need. He needed to put his friendship with Zach—his loyalty to his friends and partners— ahead of his fascination with Nicole.

Indulging in his hunger for her would only cloud his vision where she was concerned, and it was crucial that he remain clear-eyed and focused to wade through the mystery of Matthew's paternity. Maybe it was a futile hope that lying in the snow would chill him out. But Desmond didn't get out to a range often since he'd purchased the casino, so he indulged the urge now to redirect his thoughts.

With the gusts quieted for a moment, he focused on his breathing, his finger bared on the trigger. Inhale. Exhale.

Inhale. Exhale.

An empty-lung shooter, he was ready to fire when he finished the exhale, eye on the target through his scope. But an old, unwanted voice sounded in his brain as he gently squeezed off the shot.

Aim small, miss small.

Gunfire sounding, Desmond cursed himself for giving his father's voice any bandwidth in his head.

"Nice one," the tech from the ranch's gun club

called over to him from the stand. "You're just a hairsbreadth from dead center."

Which was a miss according to the man who'd dragged Desmond out hunting when he'd been far too young to handle a weapon. Securing the rifle now, he tugged off his hearing protection and levered to his feet. As he walked down the hill to return the Winchester to the tech, he saw another figure inside the covered wooden stand.

Gage Striker, one of Desmond's partners, stood off to one side. A New Zealander with a devil-may-care way about him that flew in the face of his up-tight family's political ambitions for him, Gage was a former investment banker who'd turned to angel investing, giving him more free time after years of working 24-7. Gage had recently reunited with Elena Rollins, the woman he'd nearly married six years ago until Gage's father had interfered with their re-lationship.

"Gage." Desmond greeted him with a nod before turning over his weapon to the waiting tech. "Are you waiting for the range? The crosswind is trouble, but it comes and goes."

"No." Gage waved away the offer of the rifle. "Waiting to speak to you, if you have a few min-utes." He gestured toward the ATV waiting nearby.

"I'm surprised you knew where to find me." Des-mond packed his hearing protection in the accesso-ries bag before he joined Gage in walking toward the

ATV. The snow was well packed here, the shooting range a popular guest attraction year-round.

"When you weren't at home this morning, I took a chance you'd be out here." Dropping into the driver's seat, Gage turned the key in the ignition, thankfully not remarking on Desmond's tendency to shoot when he was stressed.

It made no sense, really, since the dad he'd grown up resenting—often physically fearing—had been the one to teach him. But as time went by, his skills had surpassed his father's. And there was a comfort in being better with a firearm than your enemy. His dad had died of a heart attack nearly a decade ago, but the ugly legacy he'd left behind still resurfaced sometimes.

Desmond slid into the passenger seat, the frustration of the sleepless night still heavy on his shoulders. He didn't feel any need to share what being around Nicole was doing to him personally. There were enough more obvious reasons they were all tense this week.

"When did you get in?" Desmond withdrew his glove from his coat pocket and returned it to his shooting hand. "Is Elena with you?"

"Yes. We flew in this morning. She's been upset ever since she heard about Chiara being targeted by Alec's assistant." Gage put the ATV in gear and headed in the direction of Desmond's house. "I wanted her to stay away until we got to the bottom of this mess, but with Nicole and Matthew arriving, she booked the next flight out for us."

Gage and Elena had been in Los Angeles, where Elena still kept an apartment, but Gage resided in Silicon Valley, where they were planning to live full-time. Elena had been a fashion and lifestyle social media influencer, on a smaller scale than Chiara Campagna, but Chiara convinced her to expand her fashion design talents.

"So you're just in time for tonight's dinner with Nicole Cruz," Desmond observed, unable to leave her out of the conversation for long when she dominated his thoughts.

"Yes. Miles texted us this morning about that." Gage picked up speed as they reached a smoother road along a field they would use for grazing in the spring. As part of the ranch's green initiatives, they rotated grazing areas frequently. "But I wanted to get your thoughts on the situation before we all meet."

"On what?" Desmond grabbed the roll bar to steady himself as Gage took a bump at high speed.

"On Matthew Cruz's father. You know Chiara has been adamant that she saw Zach kissing Nicole's sister, Lana Allen, a student teacher at Dowdon."

Desmond remembered Chiara from their school days, before she'd reinvented herself with a new name for social media. Back then, Kara Marsh had attended the girls' school down the road. She'd had a crush on Zach and had been devastated to see him kissing Miss Allen the week before his death.

Had Nicole's sister really preyed on a teenager? If it was true, Zach had kept it a secret from his friends. Lana Allen might have been young at the time—just twenty years old to Zach's seventeen. But Zach had been a minor in the care of the school, so a relationship would have been criminal.

"I'm aware." Desmond's temples throbbed, the stress of wading through the past weighing heavy. Miles had told them about Chiara's revelation just days ago, but the news had been overshadowed by Vivian Fraser's arrest for stalking and hacking. "I haven't asked Nicole about it yet. I don't want to bias her toward Zach until we see what she knows first. She might have an entirely different angle on this."

Part of him still held out hope that Matthew wasn't Zach's son. That Alonzo Salazar, their old mentor, had been helping support the boy just because Lana Allen had been his student teacher and not because Alonzo had been a friend or mentor to the child's father.

"But what's your gut telling you?" Gage scrubbed a hand along his jaw, squinting through a light haze of snow that whirled through the open cab of the ATV when the treads kicked up loose powder. "Why would Zach come out as gay to us if he wasn't?"

"Damned if I know." Desmond had turned over the puzzle plenty of times and came up empty. "He could have been bisexual but didn't realize it that summer when he told us."

"But why come out at all if he wasn't certain?"

Gage shook his head, dark eyebrows furrowed as he frowned. "Zach seemed fearless to me in a lot of ways, but even for a guy who seems like he has it all together, that's a bold step. Who does that if they aren't sure?"

An uncomfortable thought occurred to him, not for the first time. "You don't think he did it to help hide an affair with a teacher?"

"Absolutely not." Gage's voice was certain. Adamant. "He wasn't deliberately deceitful."

The knot in Desmond's chest eased a fraction, Gage's faith in their friend reassuring him. He'd echoed Desmond's own long-held opinion that Zach was the best of them. They'd always looked up to him.

"And yet he kept the relationship with Lana a secret. But if Zach wasn't Matthew's father, and we know none of us are, either, who else would Alonzo Salazar have been covering for to financially support Matthew Cruz?" He asked the question aloud, but of course Gage wouldn't have any answers, either.

Riding the rest of the way in silence, Desmond hoped they'd learn more once he introduced Nicole to his friends.

And if some part of him felt defensive of her being put in the hot seat by the Mesa Falls partners, Desmond would just have to squelch it, along with all the other tangled feelings he had for Nicole.

Standing in front of Desmond's massive home on the Mesa Falls property, Nicole wondered how one person could possibly need this much space. The three-story stone-and-cedar-shingle structure perched on the edge of a small pond, with only a few wandering elk nearby for company. She'd ridden a snowmobile over from the main lodge, eager to continue her quest for answers today even though he'd texted her details about a meeting with his partners later tonight.

Did he honestly think she was going to sit idly all day when Mattie's future rested on her locating his father?

Frustrated, she pressed the button for the doorbell again, peering in through the leaded glass in the front door. She could hear the resonant sound of the chimes inside, although the place was so large she wondered if it could be heard in the farthest rooms. She pulled out her phone to text him that she was outside while she listened for signs of life within the house. But before she could open up the contact information on her screen, she heard a distant hum of a motor from somewhere behind her instead.

Stepping out from under the arched entryway, she stayed on the shoveled stone path to keep her boots out of the packed snow. The engine noise grew until she spotted a two-seater ATV heading toward her through the woods behind the pond. Pocketing her phone again, she wandered onto the back patio, where heavy outdoor furniture sat in a ring around a built-in fire pit. As the ATV neared, she spied two men in the front seat.

One of whom was definitely Desmond.

Her skin flushed despite the cold, awareness and anticipation combining to remind her that she needed to guard herself around him at all times. The heated draw was as distracting as it was compelling. Last night, as they sat outside watching the ice-skaters near the lodge, she'd been tantalized by the feel of his hand on hers. When was the last time she'd had skin-on-skin contact with any man?

The vehicle slowed near the patio, the driver parking the vehicle close to the shoveled cobblestones. A Plexiglas windscreen shielded them in front, but the low side doors had no windows, allowing her to see Desmond clearly as he unlatched the passenger side and stepped out near her.

"Nicole." His gray eyes sizzled over her with words unspoken, his attention as stirring as any touch. "I didn't know you were looking for me."

"I should have messaged you." She hadn't because she'd feared he might be avoiding her until the larger meeting with his friends.

"Nicole, this is Gage Striker." Desmond stopped beside her, gesturing toward the driver of the vehicle. "He's one of my partners you'll be seeing more of at dinner."

"Nice to meet you." She smiled politely, her manner businesslike. And although the dark-haired man with a square jaw and powerful shoulders was technically as handsome as Desmond, she found it easy to maintain her distance.

"You, too, love." He used the endearment the way some people said "friend" or "ma'am," although his New Zealand accent lent the word a different sort of charm. "Thank you for making the trip to Montana." He gave her a nod. "See you soon."

Then he pulled away, the engine humming louder for a moment before quieting as the ATV headed up the driveway toward the main lodge.

Leaving her alone with Desmond on the patio of his rustic mansion.

"Would you like to come inside?" Desmond's voice held an intimate note as he delivered the simple question.

Or was she hearing a subtext he didn't intend?

Her heart sped faster. She looked more carefully at him now, taking in details she hadn't noticed before. The crusted ice on the placket of his field jacket. His red cheeks.

"If you don't mind," she said carefully. "But if I'm interrupting your plans—"

"I have no plans other than warming up." His gloved hand brushed the small of her back through her long coat, guiding her toward a back entrance. "Let's go inside."

Her belly tightened as she moved in that direction, hoping she hadn't overestimated her ability to remain immune to this man now that she was accompanying him into his house alone. Although she was curious about what he'd been doing to leave ice down the front of his jacket, she didn't want to take things to a more personal level. Instead, she focused on the house as he reached around her to disarm the alarm and open the back door.

"This is a beautiful home." She stepped onto a three-season porch with a stone floor and firewood neatly stacked along one wall. Colorful wool blankets draped over the arm of a sofa that looked out on the snowy backyard.

"I can't take much credit for it." He reached around her to open another door into the main house. "I told a builder what I wanted in a vacation residence when we first bought the ranch and haven't spent much time here since."

She followed him into a French country kitchen with cream-colored distressed wood cabinets and a white oak floor with wide planks. A wrought iron chandelier hung over an island that dominated the room. Everything was absurdly neat, with no personal items left on countertops or photos on the wall.

He waved her through to a smaller living area that was more like a den at the back of the house. A beige rolled-arm couch sat close to a hearth built into a stone wall. A real wood fire burned in the grate behind a wrought iron screen, though the warmth came from mostly embers now. Bookshelves lined one wall while another looked out over the frozen pond and snowy yard.

"If you give me your coat, I can get you something hot to drink while you make yourself comfortable." He moved behind her to take the long, fawn-colored garment, his hands on either side of her shoulders but not yet touching.

The heat of him radiated into her all the same.

"You don't need to go to any trouble on my account," she protested, taking in the intimacy of the small room.

Why hadn't she asked him to meet her at the lodge, where there were more people around? Less temptation to look her fill at the man near her.

"It's not just for you." He lifted her coat from her shoulders and eased it down her arms. "I've been out at the rifle range this morning and I'll need something to thaw out."

For a moment she caught a hint of his scent as he stood behind her—sandalwood and musk. But before she could take a deeper breath to be sure, he moved toward the fireplace to lift a poker and stir the fire to life.

He added another log from a basket off to one side, then laid a second at an angle to the first. The dry edge of one caught fire almost immediately.

"In that case, thank you." Nicole lowered herself to sit on the couch, leaving him three-quarters of the space for when he returned.

She didn't ask him about the shooting hobby, even though she was curious about that, too. She hadn't come to Montana to make idle chitchat with Desmond Pierce, no matter how much he intrigued her. Withdrawing her phone as he left the room with her coat, Nicole pulled up her checklist of questions she wanted answered and things she needed to accomplish today.

In the kitchen, she heard him rummaging through cabinets and turning a burner on the stove. One of the items on her list was to call Matthew to make sure he'd settled back into his routine after their trip, but she didn't know how much time she had before Desmond returned.

When it seemed quiet in the kitchen, she rose from the sofa to glance at his bookshelves until he returned. Because while she didn't want to ask him personal questions directly, she couldn't deny it would be helpful to learn more about him in order to help her decide if her sister, Lana, had ever pursued a relationship with him.

It seemed impossible that her uptight step sibling who always did the right thing could have had an affair with a student her first year as a teaching assistant. Frankly, the idea flew in the face of every belief she'd ever had about high-achieving Lana.

But who else could Alonzo Salazar have been covering for when he'd arranged to send that financial support to Matthew? Her gaze skimmed the titles on the shelves—business books, guides to interior design for consumer spaces, photo collections of famous casinos. No matter that Desmond said he hadn't spent much time here, those looked like books he would have chosen. Her fingertip followed the movement of her eyes as she came to the end of a shelf and spotted a row of leather-bound volumes beneath it that looked older, the titles in faded gold leaf. A few early American playwrights, some histories of Montana, a biography of a regional artist.

Her index finger came to rest on a copy of the Kama Sutra, and her mouth went dry. Not that it mattered one way or another that he possessed a copy of the world's oldest guide to pleasure.

Of course it didn't. But that didn't stop her cheeks from flaming when he stepped into the den with a stoneware mug in each hand.

"Find anything interesting?"

Four

Well, damn.

Desmond stilled where he stood near the couch, watching the interesting play of color over Nicole's lovely features. Pink flushed her cheeks. Her breath quickened between parted lips. He could see the rapid rise and fall of her breasts through the fitted, ivory-colored sweater she wore with dark gray jeans. As he watched, her teeth sank into the fullness of her lower lip, holding it fast. And he couldn't seem to drag his gaze away from that spot, certain he felt a phantom bite on his own skin.

Apparently he hadn't needed to bother preparing hot cocoa. This woman fired up his insides just being in the same room with him.

"I was admiring your book collection," she murmured finally, long after he'd forgotten what he'd asked.

Thankfully, the words broke whatever spell her hectic color had aroused in him, forcing him to get his mind off her delectable mouth. And hell, he had no business thinking about her that way when he had a job to do as intermediary with her for the other ranch owners. He couldn't put off talking to her about the DNA test results any longer.

"I've forgotten what volumes I have here," he admitted, setting down the two stoneware mugs on a marble tray resting on the coffee table. "I read most of them during the summer we spent hashing out the ranch mission. Other than that visit, I haven't been in Mesa Falls in years."

She moved around the opposite end of the sofa from where he stood, taking a seat in the far corner. "I haven't had enough time for reading since my sister's death. My life changed so dramatically overnight." With one hand, she slid a sofa pillow onto her lap, her fingers flexing in the burgundy-colored velvet. She kept her phone held tight in the other. "I'm only just starting to get my feet underneath me again."

He couldn't help but feel a pang of empathy for her as he focused on her hands. Her fingernails were unpainted, and gold filigree bands threaded around two fingers on each hand. Chips of colored gemstones were woven into a few of them.

"I'm sorry for what you've been through." He dropped onto the sofa cushion at the other end of the couch, not wanting to crowd her. Needing distance for his own peace of mind, too. He slid the marble tray closer to her so she could reach her drink more easily. "I never lost a blood-related sibling, but the death of someone I thought of as a brother left me walking around in a fog of grief for the better part of a year."

Longer, really, since he'd felt responsible for Zach's death. All his friends did in some way. They'd failed Zach when he needed them most, because whether or not he'd intended to jump to his death, he'd definitely been upset that weekend. They'd taken the trip to try to be supportive of whatever he'd been going through. Zach hadn't wanted to discuss it, but he'd wanted to leave campus, and they'd all gone with him.

The guilt was heavy. But Desmond wouldn't keep failing him now. If there was any chance Matthew Cruz was Zach's son, Nicole needed to know about him. He'd hoped to wait for that discussion until tonight, to gauge his conversations with her in case she had other ideas for whom her sister had been seeing nine months before Matthew's birth. But with Nicole sitting in his den beside him, Desmond couldn't wait any longer.

She reached for her mug, staring at him curiously.

"Lana wasn't my sister by blood, either," she confided. Surprising him. His private investigator had only just begun to search for answers about Lana Allen. They hadn't known the connection to Nicole and Matthew until days ago, when Chiara Campagna had picked out Lana Allen in the background of a yearbook photo from Dowdon School. "Before I was born, my father married her mother to protect Lana and her mom from Lana's abusive dad."

Thoughts of Zach faded as this new information came to light. Desmond had more in common with Nicole than he ever would have suspected—the death of a sibling figure, for one thing. Domestic violence for another.

He went cold at the possibility of anyone hurting Nicole.

Or, hell, Matthew.

The idea of someone like Desmond's dad getting anywhere near this woman and the vulnerable kid she guarded, who could be Zach's son, had him shooting to his feet.

"Is he still in the picture? The abuser?" Desmond's voice hardened. He heard it but couldn't help it as he walked woodenly to the fireplace and tossed more logs on the fire. Even though he'd already done that when they first came in the room.

The twitchy need to move was too strong to ignore.

"No." Nicole set her mug back down. "God, no. Lana never saw him again. And I kept an eye out at her funeral just in case her dad could have somehow heard about her passing, but there was no one."

"You're sure?" He ground his teeth, hating the way his own past with his father could still freeze him from the inside out.

He used one log to move the end of another one already in the fireplace, sending sparks onto the stone hearth. The scent of burning applewood intensified.

"Positive. My father was deep in his own grief at the memorial service, but if Lana's father had been in attendance, Dad would have recognized the guy." She scooched forward on the couch, her auburn hair spilling over one shoulder as she moved. "Why?"

He had no intention of bringing up his own past with his father. Sebastian Pierce had moved on long ago, leaving Desmond's mother once he'd taken as much of her estate as he could get his hands on. If only the guy had been just a thief and not a violent thug. Desmond had more than made up for her financial losses, but he couldn't give her back the emotional security and sense of self his father had stolen. With an effort, he tamped down the old anger to refocus their conversation.

"I'm just thinking of Matthew's safety." Rising again, Desmond paced around the den, pausing in front of a small, leather-topped wooden desk. He opened the center drawer to retrieve an envelope. "And in regard to your nephew, I've heard back about the paternity tests." Withdrawing the envelope, he laid it on the marble tray between their mugs. "We already had the results from Alonzo Salazar's heirs, and there is no genetic tie between Salazar and Matthew, either."

"I never suspected Mr. Salazar. Lana looked up to him, but he was much older than her." Nicole lifted her drink, pursing her lips to blow gently across the hot surface.

His mouth went dry as he imagined the cooling stream of air over his heated skin. For a moment, he simply stared at her, wondering what was happening to him that this woman could make him lose perspective so fast.

When she raised her warm-chocolate eyes to his, he realized he'd been quiet too long, lost in thoughts of her. Steeling himself, he forced his brain back to the painful task to come.

"We're in agreement there. None of my partners thought Alonzo would have violated a professional code of conduct that way." Desmond would forever be grateful to the only teacher at Dowdon to have an inkling of what they'd been through after Zach's death. "But I have the other paternity test results, as well. There were no genetic matches between Matthew and any of the Mesa Falls partners, either."

Confusion clouded her gaze before her focus went to the documents he'd placed before her.

"You've already heard back?" Setting the mug down, she thumbed through the papers briefly, then huffed out a breath as she set them on the couch. "What am I even doing here if none of you are Matthew's father? I'm back to square one in my search."

"Not exactly." He braced himself for the pain of what had to come next—talking about Zach, whose death had rewritten his whole life and everything he knew about himself. "The friend I mentioned earlier—the one I said wasn't related by blood, but he was like a brother to me?" At her nod, he continued. "Zach Eldridge went to Dowdon with us. He died in a cliff-jumping accident fourteen years ago, but we've heard recently that he might have had a relationship with Lana."

For a long moment, Nicole stared at him blankly. "Fourteen years ago?"

"He died the autumn before Matthew's birth." Desmond knew the boy's birth date from the private investigator's files. It was seven months after Zach's death.

Blinking fast, Nicole shifted aside the sofa pillow. "Do you have a photo of him? Of Zach?" She rose to her feet, still appearing a bit dazed as she hugged herself with her arms. "Was this friend your same age?"

Leaning a shoulder against the stone fireplace surround, Desmond withdrew his phone to search for an image while the flames in the hearth popped, the logs shifting.

"I have a photo somewhere. He was in the same grade as me, although he was a year older." Desmond had never spoken about his friend to anyone outside the group he'd attended school with. "Maturity-wise, however, he was light-years older than all of us."

"It just seems entirely out of character for my perfectionist sister to have an affair with a student." She twisted one of the gold rings around her pointer finger, an agitated gesture as she came to a stop in front of him. "No matter how mature your friend was, it's tough to imagine Lana being tempted into a deeply unethical relationship that could have resulted in prison time. I couldn't get past that part whenever I thought about one of the Mesa Falls owners as being Matthew's father either. It doesn't seem like something Lana would have done."

"I understand. A relationship like that is upsetting to consider. But it could explain why my friend was so upset that last weekend before he died." Desmond continued scrolling, wishing he had better answers for her. Answers that wouldn't bring Nicole more pain in a year that had already been beyond difficult for her.

"I'm just surprised I haven't even heard of him before now. Zach Eldridge," she mused aloud, testing out the name.

"He was in the foster system, and his death was problematic for both the state and the school. News of it was kept to a bare minimum, and never in connection with Dowdon."

Zach had taught Desmond how to fight. A lesson that had meant the difference between merely surviving his home life and getting rid of his bastard father for good. The only sad part of the day Sebastian

Pierce packed up his bags forever was that Desmond hadn't been able to share it with Zach.

"Thank you for helping me," Nicole said suddenly, her hand falling lightly on his forearm. "Especially now that you and all the other Mesa Falls owners can't be Mattie's father. It's kind of you to continue to help."

Her touch affected him like a lightning strike. But damned if her deep brown gaze wasn't just as compelling. Maybe even more so.

"If my mentor risked his name and reputation to write a book that would support Matthew's upbringing, then the boy is important to me. To all of us at Mesa Falls. Period. I just wish Alonzo was still alive so we could ask him what he knew."

He passed over his phone with an image of Zach standing next to a painting he'd done at a school art show. "Do you recognize him?"

Nicole took the device with unsteady hands.

Part of her unease came from this latest development in her search for Matthew's father. But a bigger share was the awareness that lit through her just from standing beside Desmond in the cozy room that smelled pleasantly of wood smoke. Touching him hadn't been wise since her fingertips still hummed from the contact.

Did he feel any portion of this electricity? Maybe if she had more experience with men, she would have a better answer to that. But seeing the way her sister's plans for her future had evaporated once she'd gotten pregnant had had a dramatic impact on Nicole at an impressionable age. She'd avoided boys altogether, gathering none of the experience most girls had by the time they went to college. Even then, Nicole had focused on her studies. Afterward, her few dating choices had been purely practical, lacking any of the charged sensation she felt around the man beside her.

Angling Desmond's phone screen to see the photo better, she felt her breath catch at the sight of a young man she did indeed recognize. Brown eyes full of laughter stared back at her from an angular face with dark hair that swept over thick, straight eyebrows. He stood on a grassy hilltop flanked by a younger version of Desmond Pierce, whose gray eyes were as chilly and forbidding as his friend's were warm and inviting. The contrast made her all the more curious about Desmond, even as she wondered how his friend figured into her sister's life.

"To think he's only a few years older than Matthew is now," Nicole murmured aloud, her brain full of questions about Lana's past and the secrets she'd kept. "I don't see a resemblance between them though, do you?"

"Nicole." Desmond's voice was close to her. The lone word spoken like a demand. "You *do* recognize him, don't you?"

She was too rattled to think through potential consequences, too intrigued to be cautious. Besides, Desmond could apparently read her well, so she didn't bother holding back.

"I saw them together the summer before school started," she admitted, her gaze veering between the two faces in the photo. "It didn't occur to me he might be a student. I though he was a local."

"Zach went to an art program that summer." The words sounded pulled from him as if by an effort, and she recognized that even now, talking about his friend was painful. "He was on campus then. Where did you see him?"

"He walked her home once." In her mind's eye, she could still see Lana smiling up at the tall, broad-shouldered young man. "We lived off-campus even though my father did gardening work for Dowdon. When the weather was nice, Lana liked taking walks into the nearby village."

At least, she assumed that's where Lana had been coming from on the day Nicole recalled. She would have paid better attention if she'd ever guessed her sister's life and the company she kept would be of so much importance now that Nicole had guardianship of Lana's only child.

"Did they seem…close?" Desmond asked, studying her face as if the clues he sought might be written there.

"Maybe?" She bit her lip, wishing she could recall more than a vague impression of her sister flirting with the guy. "I was still young, so I might not have understood the nuances of their body language."

"And that was the only time you saw Zach?" Desmond pressed, forcing her to explain herself.

He stood close enough to touch. Close enough that if she breathed deeply she could catch a hint of his sandalwood scent.

"That was the only time I'd seen them *together*," she insisted, wanting justice done. "But I saw Zach alone at an art show near the end of summer."

His eyes flicked to hers, stirring the uneasy interest again, the one that made her insides ache and her skin feel twitchy.

"What does your gut tell you, Nicole? Do you think your sister had an affair with my friend?"

Her stomach knotted. That actually would account for a lot of strange things that had happened that year. Lana had quit her college program without finishing her student teaching. Then she'd moved away suddenly, taking work in a library in Oregon. Once Nicole had learned about her sister's pregnancy, she'd assumed that was why, although it hadn't really accounted for not getting her teaching degree when she'd been so close to finishing. But if she'd had an illicit affair?

It made her ill to think about it. And she wasn't ready to share that with Desmond. Plus, as much as she wanted answers, she also feared what she might find out about the other side of Matthew's family. What if another legal relation—someone with an actual blood tie to the boy—wanted to take Mattie away from her?

"I don't know. Can we get a DNA sample from one of Zach's relatives?"

"He doesn't have any that we know about," Desmond told her flatly, his eyes fixed on her. "That's one reason he was in the foster system. He lived on the streets for three months after his father died, but then child services picked him up. He attended Dowdon on a scholarship."

"How sad for him," she murmured, more to herself than Desmond. She paced away from him, thinking out loud, her finger running idly over one of the rows of books on a nearby shelf. "Although it makes sense that Alonzo Salazar would pitch in to help Lana's child if he knew the father of her baby was dead and there were no relatives who could help my sister support him."

"Perhaps." Desmond's noncommittal answer made her look up sharply to peer at him over her shoulder.

"You don't agree?" She halted at the end of the bookshelf, her fingers pausing to rest on a leather volume.

"I just wonder how Salazar knew your sister's circumstances in the first place." Desmond followed her across the den, stopping beside her. "She left school suddenly and we never heard any more about her."

His nearness made her heart race faster. She glanced down and away from him, her gaze falling on—of all things—that too-intriguing Kama Sutra book she'd noticed earlier. She wrapped her arms around herself, needing more barriers between her and the man who affected her so strongly.

"Lana argued with my dad and moved out over Thanksgiving break. Then, my father packed us up and moved us to a new town after that." At just fourteen years old, Nicole had been furious at the time—at her sister as much as her dad. Little did she know how difficult the situation had been for both of them, too. "I never understood why, but I thought it had something to do with my sister's refusal to name the child's father."

Nicole's parents had already been divorced by then, but the move had made it difficult to see her mother. Not that her astronomer mom had ever made great efforts to see her, since she was attached to her work more than her family.

"Lana must have left school the same time Zach died. No wonder we didn't hear anything about her pregnancy," Desmond mused aloud, his gray eyes wandering over her, missing nothing. "That must have been a difficult time for you."

The empathy in his gaze seemed to tug her toward him. Blinking, she told herself it was an illusion. She didn't have any reason to trust Desmond. And she sure wasn't trusting her own instincts right now when her every atom was pulling her toward the man in front of her. She wanted to kiss him, she realized with total clarity and more than a little surprise.

She wanted to fist her fingers in his shirtfront and drag him the rest of the way to her before rising up on her toes and brushing her lips over his for a long, thorough taste.

"Desmond." His name escaped her on a sigh so needy-sounding she wished she could call it back. Appalled at herself, she covered her mouth with her fingers for a moment while his eyes darkened. Her hand fell away from her lips to try and steer the conversation away from the awkward moment. "That is—I could use some fresh air."

Oh, that was smooth, she chastised herself. Her heart pounded harder, and she imagined her face growing redder with each beat.

"That's probably a good idea," he agreed in a reasonable tone even as he reached for her. "But I need to do something first."

When his fingers landed on her shoulders, she knew she wasn't alone in feeling the electric connection between them. He must feel it, too, or he wouldn't look at her this way right now. Like he was a starving man, and she was a gourmet meal he needed to devour. Yesterday.

So she didn't question what he needed to do, because whatever it was, she wanted him to do it. Immediately.

Preferably with his hands, his mouth and his delectable hard body, too.

But then his lips crashed down on hers and she couldn't think at all. She could only sink into the most sinfully hot kiss she'd ever known.

Strong arms enveloped her, pressing her close.

Her nerve endings flamed to red-hot life, set afire by all that taut masculine strength. The scent of his aftershave teased her nostrils while his lips coaxed hers wide, his tongue sweeping over hers until she swore she could feel that same sensual caress in her most intimate places. She shivered with the thought, her nipples puckering into tight points.

He backed her up a step, guiding her toward a wall that steadied her when her knees felt weak. Her head tipped back as she offered her neck for another kiss. He licked his way lower, the heady feel of his mouth at her throat calling a whimper from her.

She wrapped her arms around his neck, all sense of caution lost when he edged back a few inches from her, his eyes dark with desire. For a moment, they breathed each other in from that close distance as the world slowly returned.

Desmond's eyelids fell shut for a moment. When they flicked open again, there was a coolness in their depths.

"Fresh air might not be enough to quench the fire." He levered away from her but took one of her hands in his as he led her toward the door. "We'd better keep an eye out for a snowbank."

Five

Desmond didn't have a plan other than trying to get himself under control again. Something that wouldn't happen if he remained in close quarters with Nicole another minute.

That kiss.

He hadn't wanted it to ever end. Even now, as he retraced their steps from when they entered the house to retrieve their coats, he felt the residual flames her touch had incited. Heat roared through him while the need to taste her again was an insistent ache. Knowing he didn't dare help her into her long overcoat for fear of peeling all her clothes off instead, Desmond passed her the garment before punching his fists through the sleeves of his own. Then, on second thought, he returned to the kitchen, grabbing an insulated picnic hamper from the pantry and bringing it to the Sub-Zero, where he transferred a package with the day's catering delivery into the basket.

"Would you like a hand?" Nicole offered as she pulled her outerwear tighter around her, the belt accenting her narrow waist.

"No, thanks." His gaze skipped over her, his eyes lingering on curves that even layers of wool and cashmere didn't hide. "I just thought I'd bring something to eat."

If he was feeding one hunger, he couldn't very well act on the other, more insistent one.

"Where are we going?" she asked, absently twining the ends of her hair into a braid that started at her shoulder.

"I'd love to show you around the ranch on horseback," he offered, suggesting the first thing that came to mind that would keep them out of the house.

"Sounds wonderful. I love to ride." She trailed her fingers over the lapel of her long overcoat. "I'm not dressed for it, though."

His gaze followed the motion of her hands, his brain mentally replacing her palms with his. Hell, he could practically feel her just imagining it. He ground his teeth together and charged toward the back door.

"There are extra jackets in the tack room," he said with a growl in his voice, recognizing his surly manners and powerless to soften them.

He held the door for her, though, arming the alarm system behind them as they left the house and started toward the stable. The structure was small compared to the horse barns near the lodge or the even bigger, utilitarian building situated on the portion of Mesa Falls that served as the operations base for the working ranch.

But the three stalls inside a cedar-shingle building were more than enough for Desmond's needs. He led Nicole into the stable, the scent of fresh hay and horse mingling with the fragrant cedar of the walls.

"What beautiful animals." Nicole stopped at the stall door of a pretty buckskin mare, and stroked her nose. "What are their names?"

"That's Spirit, and the chestnut is Sundancer. These are two of my favorites." He paused by the stall to greet the animal. "A ranch hand brought them over from the main lodge's stables last night. I've only been on-site at Mesa Falls for three days myself, so I'm still getting settled." It hadn't helped that he'd been preoccupied as hell ever since arriving.

He'd been intrigued by Nicole after one phone call. Then, after the accidental video chat while she'd been in bed, Desmond's fascination with her had grown exponentially. Spending time with her in person now—alone—was killing his resolve to keep his distance.

"I'm sure the transition between life at the casino and the ranch is considerable." She cooed at the horse and tipped her forehead to the mare's. "But I can help prep if you show me the tack room."

Desmond set the insulated picnic hamper on a shelf by the door and walked to the back of the stable. "You don't need to do that."

"I insist." She surprised him by following him toward the pegboard where the bridles were lined up on metal hooks. "My father raised me to care for animals that served me."

He passed her a lined canvas jacket for riding, and she eased out of her more formal cashmere and wool coat. While his instincts as a gentleman barked at him to assist her, he still didn't trust himself not to kiss her again so soon after the scorching clinch in the den. He'd memorized the exquisite feel of her pressed against him, and he burned to recreate that moment, only with less clothes between them.

Preferably none.

He busied himself with the bridles, pulling two down from the hooks while he tried to forget the swell of her breasts, the rapid tattoo of her heartbeat and the swift intake of her breath when he'd swept his tongue into her mouth that first time.

"Your dad sounds like a good man." He cursed the harsh note in his voice as he passed her the bridles and carried the saddles himself. "You said he was a gardener?"

He stopped outside the stalls, hefting the saddles onto the racks near the cross-tie points in the aisle.

Nicole laid one of the bridles near the rack and kept the other one in hand as he led Spirit out of her stall.

"Yes. He was head gardener at Dowdon for five years." Nicole helped him secure the animal in the cross ties, then cooed to the mare while she slid the bridle over her head. "I wasn't excited to move there when he took the job, since my parents had just divorced, and my mom made it clear she wasn't seeking any visitation rights. But I came to like the town."

"Wow. That had to have been rough. How old were you?" He ran a brush over the mare's back, curious about her.

"Nine. Mom is a renowned astronomer." She hesitated.

At her pause, he stopped brushing the horse to see her face. She looked out one of the open windows, her teeth nibbling at her lower lip in a gesture that made his throat go dry.

When she continued, she turned her dark eyes on him, and he set down the brush to lay a saddle blanket over the mare.

"I'm proud of her. She leads her own research team studying solar magnetics. But it wasn't always easy to take second place behind the sun." She reached over to smooth the blanket while he retrieved the tooled leather saddle. "I've vowed to make sure Matthew knows he comes first with me. Always."

He couldn't help but respect the conviction in her voice. His own mother hadn't been able to put him first, either, because Sebastian Pierce had demanded her full attention at all times. What would it have been like to grow up with a parent who advocated for him?

"Matthew is lucky to have you in his life." Desmond bent to tighten the cinches, grateful for something to keep his hands busy when he wanted them on Nicole. "There aren't many people who could have devoted as much time to finding answers about his parentage as you have."

"Thank you. But it's getting to be *too* much time." She helped him unfasten the cross ties now that Spirit was ready to ride. "I guess I'm fortunate to free-lance my graphic design skills so I can take the extra weeks away from the job, but if I want to pay Matthew's next tuition bill, I'll need to return to work soon."

He brooded on that while he led Sundancer from his stall to saddle him. He didn't want to offend her by intruding on her finances, but since they affected a child who could be Zach's son, he couldn't keep silent.

"What about the legacy from Salazar's book? I thought the nominee service that forwarded profits had instructions to continue payments after his death?" Securing the horse, Desmond repeated the procedure with Sundancer while Nicole held Spirit's reins near the barn door.

"It does." She spoke stiffly. Unwillingly? "But I can't in good conscience continue to let Matthew accept the income from a book that ripped apart a family and profited on a scandal that caused real people harm."

He understood her reasoning but her scruples weren't going to give the family depicted in *Hollywood Newlyweds* back their lives before the scandal. He'd have to convince her to continue taking the funds Alonzo had worked hard to ensure could support the boy. An argument he'd save for the next time he needed distance from those too-compelling dark eyes, or the siren's call of her full lips.

For now, he adjusted the saddle and sufficed to say, "If Matthew is Zach's son, he's entitled to a portion of Mesa Falls. This whole place was built as a way to remember Zach, so it's only natural we'd share it with his son. That would ensure Matthew's financial future."

He didn't need to check with his partners about that. They would insist upon it as much as he would. They'd rewrite the deed into sevenths instead of sixths to include Zach's heir.

"That's a big *if* we may never be able to prove." Nicole stared at him with challenge in her eyes, her chin tilted up. "And no matter what we learn about his parentage, I'm not going to relinquish my spot as his primary guardian no matter the financial incentive. It's probably best we're clear on that from the start."

Her voice vibrated with emotion he hadn't expected. But before he could assure her that wasn't his intent, she was leading Spirit from the barn, her head high and her back ramrod straight.

Damn.

He'd wanted to cool things off between them. He hadn't meant to send her into deep freeze.

Steeling himself for riding beside her for the afternoon, he told himself it was better this way. Safer for all parties if he kept Nicole at arm's length. But the part of him that remembered how she tasted sure as hell mourned the loss.

Nicole fumed for the first twenty minutes of the ride, aggravated by the idea of the wealthy and powerful ranch partners involving themselves in Matthew's life. Yet, as she eyed the Bitterroot River from a high vantage point above the valley, she admitted the fresh, pine-scented air had helped ease some of her indignation over the next hour. Seated on Spirit's back with the calls of woodpeckers and kestrels in the trees above, she soaked in the natural beauty of western Montana, still dusted with snow, thinking how much Matthew would enjoy this place.

Ahead of her, Desmond reined in his mount, forcing her to slow Spirit's trot to a walk. Her host had spoken little during the tour of the ranch, but she hadn't required a guide to observe the appeal of the picturesque vistas.

"Are you hungry yet?" he asked, breaking a long silence.

Her stomach growled in a reply she was surprised he couldn't hear even a few yards ahead of her.

"I wouldn't mind something to eat." She glanced around the trees for a comfortable place to rest. "Should we stop?"

"There's a tree house up ahead if you're game to try it out." He nodded toward the north in the direction they were already moving.

"A tree house?" She couldn't hide her skepticism as she peered around again, wondering if she'd missed a residence. She remembered all of the owners had homes on the Mesa Falls land, though none of them had been built close to the others. "Way out here?"

"Yes." He shifted his weight in the saddle, cueing the sleek chestnut he rode to pick up the pace again. "We're almost there."

By the time he halted again, she'd given up keeping an eye out for a structure. Now, she looked up as she slowed her horse.

They stood surrounded by trees, the heavy limbs branching in all directions making a thick network overhead even without leaves. Yet ahead of her, she spied the underside of a two-story structure perched between four maples, a cedar staircase climbing through the trunks and then forming a walkway that circled the coolest tree house she'd ever seen. On closer inspection she could tell the lower level was an open-air deck with a table and chairs. Above that, a snug house of cedar with black-painted shutters looked like something out of a fairy tale. A few different rooflines gave the structure visual interest, with a wide peak over the hobbit-size front door, a dormer on one side and a connected mini-building that looked like a gatehouse tucked into the V of heavy tree branches to the west.

"Wow." She breathed the word reverently, charmed in spite of her determination to keep Desmond at arm's length. It was hard to hang on to her anger with him when it felt like she'd just entered Wonderland. "Is this some kind of retreat for ranch guests?"

"No." Swinging a leg over Sundancer's back, Desmond dropped to the ground. "The builder who designed my house talked me into using the left-over materials on this. He gave me a deal because he wanted to test out a new blueprint."

"It looks like something Hansel and Gretel would find in the forest." Following his lead, she slid off Spirit and secured the horse next to Desmond's.

"I'm hoping no witches have taken up residence since the last time I was here." He unclipped the insulated bag from his saddle and tucked it under one arm before waving her toward the tree house. "But let me know if you want me to go in first and clear the building, just in case."

She laughed until it occurred to her maybe bears could be up there. Wrapping her arms around herself, she scanned the place again, looking for signs of movement around the open deck on the lower level.

"That's not such a bad idea." She hurried to keep up with him as they crossed the soft bed of pine needles, the snow cover thin beneath the trees. "Don't you have a lot of wild animals in Montana? My father might have raised me with an appreciation of the natural world, but I'm still more of a city girl at heart."

"Mesa Falls has worked hard to bring back more of the animal population with our conservation efforts, so we're proud of the fact that there are more wild animals here than ten years ago." He waited for her at the base of the cedar stairs, the wind ruffling his dark hair. With the high color in his cheeks from the outdoor air, he looked at home here. More relaxed.

And very appealing.

Her heart thrummed faster as she reached his side to peer up into his gray eyes. "Don't wild animals bother the cattle?"

A grin pulled at his lips. "The elk and antelope can peacefully coexist with ranch animals. But I'll go make sure there are no wolves waiting for you up here."

Her gaze tracked his progress, lingering on the way denim hugged his thighs as he climbed. Her pulse fluttered at the thought of being alone with him again, even as she reminded herself that she should be on guard around him. All the reminding in the world wasn't easing the magnetic draw of the man.

When they reached the lower level with the open deck, she saw the small table and chairs that would be perfect for an outdoor meal. Yet Desmond didn't pause there. Rounding a corner, he continued up the next flight of stairs toward the main building. The scents of cedar and pine permeated the air until they reached the front door, where he entered a code into a security panel.

"You can't possibly have electricity out here," she exclaimed, glancing around from her higher vantage point to see if there were other buildings close by. But even up here, she could only see more trees.

"I assure you, I do." Opening the front door, he stood back to admit her. "It cost a small fortune to run the underground cable out there, but this way if we ever want to rent out the space to guests, we'll have the option."

She stepped into a miniature living room, complete with hardwood floor and a small wood stove built against a river-stone hearth. A low leather sofa sat before it, with an antique steamer chest for a cocktail table. Behind the living area, a small kitchen with a two-burner cooktop and wet bar area was partially surrounded by a countertop with three wooden stools.

A heavy chandelier hung over it all, drawing her attention up to the high ceiling, where a ladder led to a loft bed that looked out the dormer window she'd seen from outside.

But on the main floor, to one side, she saw the hall that must lead to the second building built to resemble a gatehouse. Through the open door, she could see a larger bedroom with what looked like a queen-size bed, and a connected bath area.

Her attention returned to the bed, heat streaking through her. Momentarily robbing her of her voice.

Thankfully, Desmond continued to speak as he closed the door behind him. "We'd need to convert the wood stove to a gas model if we let guests stay here. But for now, I prefer a real wood fire." He lowered the picnic hamper to the counter in the kitchen and strode the few steps to the cast iron unit, where he tossed in a few logs and some kindling from a nearby basket.

Shaking herself out of her inappropriate thoughts about testing the bed, Nicole's cheeks heated as she darted toward the food he'd brought.

"Guests would love to stay here. Especially kids. There's something so fanciful about the design." Peeling off the lined canvas jacket she'd borrowed from Desmond, she pulled things out of the hamper in a hurry, needing to redirect her brain. A variety of sandwiches were individually wrapped and neatly labeled. There was also a fruit plate and a large bottle of sparkling water. She found glassware in a cabinet under the counter, then poured water for both of them. "Matthew would think this was the coolest thing ever."

Desmond was quiet for a moment while he struck a match to light a twisted mound of kindling.

Then she recalled their exchange back at his house had been about Matthew—about whether or not they'd be able to prove the boy's relationship to Zach Eldridge. Would she ever bring Matthew here if he was related to Desmond's friend, knowing what a strong allegiance Desmond felt for his long-ago roommate? Or would she refuse to bring Matthew precisely because the Mesa Falls partners might use their wealth and influence to interfere in her guardianship? She was only just beginning to know Desmond. And she didn't know his friends at all.

Lost in a tangle of worries, she hadn't heard Desmond approach until he suddenly covered her hand with his. The warmth of that simple gesture called her from the swirl of questions she couldn't answer. It seemed like all she'd done was worry since her sister's death. For this one moment, with Desmond's hand on hers, she couldn't help but feel a comfort that—right now, at least—she wasn't alone.

"Nicole?" He stood close to her in the small kitchen, his big body taking up all the room.

Or maybe just all her thoughts.

His grip tightened ever so slightly on the back of her hand, the touch reassuring and inciting at the same time. With just that one simple contact, she remembered the way he'd kissed her back at his house. Like he couldn't get enough of her.

How ironic they'd ridden all this way to escape the intimacy, only to dive right back into it at the slightest touch. Clearing her throat, she tried to make an answer.

"I'm—" *Drowning in desire.* She couldn't tell him

that, though. She waited for her brain to start working again, to think about anything else besides memories of his mouth on hers.

His smoke-colored eyes darkened as he seemed to read her thoughts. His nostrils flared, his chest rising and falling harder, as if he'd been running.

"I assure you, I am, too," he muttered under his breath, skimming a hand along her cheek to cup her face and turn it up to his. He tunneled his fingers into her hair, lifting it from her back and twisting the length around his hand. "Whatever you're feeling right now, I'm so right there with you."

Her scalp tingled from his touch. Her skin was suddenly too tight. A wicked heat curled through her belly, pooling deep inside her. She pulled in a sharp breath that tasted like wood smoke and Desmond. She remembered all too well the flavor of his kiss. Her gaze dipped to his mouth, longing thick in her veins.

"How did you know what I was thinking?" she asked, her fingers trailing up the front of the fitted olive-green Henley he wore, her touch dipping and rising along a roller coaster of hard-muscled ridges until she splayed her palm on his broad, warm chest.

"I didn't." His free hand curved around her waist, his fingers skimming her back while his thumb rode the waistband of her jeans just below the hem of her sweater. It circled the spot idly. "I just felt the temperature spike in the room when you looked at me."

Her throat was too dry to answer. She was out

of her depth with him. She only knew she needed his kiss.

But he didn't close the rest of the slight distance between them, even though the heat kept rising. Confusion clouded her thoughts.

"Desmond." Her hand fisted in his shirt. Restless. Needy. "Please."

He tipped his forehead to hers, his skin even hotter than hers.

"Please what, Nicole," he urged her, lowering his lips to her ear to speak directly into it. "Just tell me what you want. I need the words."

The huff of his breath on her sensitized skin sent a shiver trembling through her. She canted toward him, her breasts brushing the solid wall of his chest in a way that sent pleasure streaking through her.

"Kiss me," she demanded, unable to think of anything else. "Kiss me again like you can't get enough."

Six

Nicole suspected she'd lost her mind along with her tenuous control, hardly recognizing the sultry command in her voice.

But she couldn't regret it. Not when Desmond edged back to look at her and she caught the moment that his gray eyes turned molten silver before lowering to fix on her mouth. One hand cupped the curve of her hip, the other settling on the back of her head to pull her to him. Then she sank into him.

His lips molded to hers, teasing and tasting. Exploring hers like new, uncharted terrain. Sensation fluttered in her belly, her fingers twisting in the fabric of his cotton shirt as if she could pull him any closer. Then he nipped her lower lip, sending pleasure arrowing through her while she gasped at the feel of his teeth. He licked the spot, soothing the sweet sting before his tongue slid inside her.

And she was lost.

She disappeared in that kiss, her mouth the center of a deep longing she hadn't known existed until he took his place there, tilting her head to perfect the angle of their joining. Making her melt. A moan escaped her, a soft, needy whimper she couldn't have hidden if she'd tried. Her knees went limp, her body trembling with shivers of anticipation. Want.

Luckily, his arm banded around her waist then or she might have slid to the floor. She couldn't have held herself up, not with this tumultuous hunger cartwheeling around inside her.

Desmond's hold tightened, sealing her hips to his, acquainting her with how much he wanted her. A lot.

A whole lot.

She wound her arms around him then, not just to anchor herself, but to ensure his lips remained where she needed them. Although, as heat seared through the rest of her body, there were other parts clamoring for that talented mouth, too. She craved that kiss everywhere, her brain too fevered to consider anything but how good it would feel. She'd been in survival mode so long. Grieving. Hurting.

She needed this hot forgetting. This burning away of everything else but addictive pleasure. His tongue stroked hers, sucking, demanding more. And she gave. Meeting his thrusts, dueling. When a low groan rumbled through his wide, hard chest, her nipples beaded to tight, aching points.

He broke the kiss abruptly, but his hands remained on her. The warm huff of his breath tickled her wet lips as he stared down into her eyes.

"If we keep this up, it's not going to end at just kissing." His voice, passion-roughened and deep, vibrated his chest and hers. "Tell me now if you're not okay with that, Nicole."

That he checked in with her was a credit to him. Swallowing hard, she couldn't find it in herself to put the brakes on an escape she needed. Desperately.

"I'm...very okay with that." She gave a jerky nod. Not because she was uncertain. Only because any movement that didn't involve fanning the flames between them felt awkward. Unnatural. "Just please, don't stop."

Later, maybe she would regret letting the depth of her need show in that hungry plea. But she couldn't possibly regret accepting the gift of his touch, just this once, when she needed to lose herself.

This. Woman.

Desmond's breath whooshed out of his lungs like a wind tunnel, taking any reservation along with it. Nicole might not *want* to desire him—he'd seen her hesitation in her fast retreat after their kiss earlier—but there was no arguing that she felt the same incendiary attraction that was burning him up from the inside now.

He would have backed off at the slightest hesitation. But her request was clear. Definite. And he had no intention of denying her when he wanted her every bit as much and more.

"Nothing would give me more pleasure than fulfilling that request." Instead of untangling her arms from around his neck—he liked them right there—he bent to lift her, hauling her body higher against his.

Gripping the backs of her thighs, he wrapped her legs around his waist to carry her to the nearest bed.

Her hum of approval pleased him almost as much as the warmth of her body where it met his. Every step he took sent mind-numbing friction between them until it took all his restraint not to back her against the nearest wall and take what they both wanted. Instead, his fingers flexed, cupping her hips to hold her steady as he turned sideways to enter the bedroom.

Don't stop.

Her dictate circled in his head, his very own sensual mantra. He had no intention of stopping until her beautiful body came apart in his arms. Until she gasped and clung to him, giving him everything.

Securing her with one arm, he dragged her creamy-colored sweater up and off her with his other. The sight of her full breasts wrapped in ivory lace would have tempted a saint, which he most definitely was not. He tugged down one strap and then the other, gaze fixed on the swell of her flesh above the cups.

He used his free hand to trail a finger down the soft valley between her breasts. "I've been seeing this spot on the backs of my eyelids every time I close my eyes. Even when I blink." He lifted his eyes to see her watching him intently, her breathing as shallow and erratic as his. "Ever since you picked up your phone for that video call, all sleep-tousled and sexy as hell, the need to see you that way again has been a fever in me."

Gently, he lowered her to the bed, cradling her back as she hit the pillowy white duvet, red hair spilling out to either side. A fantasy come to life.

"You have an advantage over me, then." Unlinking her fingers from behind his neck, she skimmed both palms down his chest and then slid cool fingers beneath the hem of his shirt. "You've seen more of me than I have of you."

Satisfaction vibrated through him that she wanted more, even as her light touch sent a blistering wave of heat over his skin. Both stunned and grateful she'd said yes to this, he wouldn't question his good fortune. He reached behind him to tug his shirt up and off, grinding his teeth against the surge of need that made him want to sink into her now. But he forced himself to take his time. If this one encounter was all he ever got with Nicole, he would make it memorable.

But he hadn't counted on her lifting up to sit on the bed in front of him while he knelt between her thighs. And he sure hadn't counted on her tongue darting out to lick a path down his naked chest. Because both those things distracted him from his plans for her.

"Damn." He breathed the word on a long exhale, hardly daring to move while she worked the fastening on his jeans and lowered the zipper.

It took every shred of his disintegrating control to move her hand away from him before she stroked him through the cotton of his boxers. Especially with her lips still gliding damp kisses just below his hip. But he captured her fingers and somehow managed to lever himself off the bed.

"Don't move," he warned her, laying a kiss on her sexy auburn waves. "I need to find protection for us."

Charging into the small bath area off the bedroom, he hoped like hell there were condoms in there. He'd had a housekeeping service refresh the tree house before his visit, and he knew there were fresh towels and sheets. But he couldn't recall what he would have ordered for personal supplies. His eyes landed on a package. Seizing the box, he scanned for an expiration date, hoping against hope.

And...*yes*. Still good.

Packet in hand, he returned to the bed, weaving around an actual limb of the maple tree that grew up through the room. Then, catching sight of Nicole, he almost swallowed his tongue.

Her back to him, she stood by the bed, her hips in midshimmy to ease off the gray denim jeans she wore. An ivory-colored lace thong graced the curve of her hip, the fabric covering little and firing the need to have her under him. Over him. All around him.

"Let me." He set the condom on the bed and took pleasure in dragging the denim down her thighs.

She steadied herself on his shoulders, the silken fall of her hair brushing his back when he leaned down. On his way back up, he kissed the skin just inside her hip, inhaling the fragrance of coconut soap or maybe something she used on her skin. She smelled delicious, and damned if he didn't want to eat her all up.

But she pushed him back onto the mattress and he let himself fall, mesmerized by the sight of her taking control over him.

"It's been a long time for me," she murmured in his ear, her breasts grazing his chest as she reached for the condom on the bed near him. "I need...this. You."

"Then I should help," he reasoned aloud, wrapping her in his arms and reversing their positions. "For expedience's sake. I'm not sure I can keep it together if you're the one to put that condom on me. It's been a while for me, too."

Just the thought of her hands on him that way was enough to send a tremor through his muscles. He stripped off the rest of his clothes, mindful of her avid gaze, and rolled on the condom without delay. He left her panties in place while he joined her on the bed, though, dragging a knuckle down the center of them, gratified to find her every bit as ready as he was.

Still, he couldn't forget what she'd said about it being a long time since she'd been with anyone. He would make certain this felt good for her. Better than good. The need to imprint himself on her memory shouldn't have been so imperative, yet he couldn't deny it.

"Desmond." She gripped his wrist, steering him, her breathing faster. Edgy.

"Trust me," he said into her ear, slipping his fingers beneath the lace and watching her expression in the gilded touch of sun streaming through a high window. "I know exactly where I'm going."

She let go of him then. Both with her fingers and with the rest of her body. Relaxing a fraction, she bit her lower lip, her eyelids fluttering as he found the touches she liked most. He kissed her cheek, and her lips parted on a breathy moan. She was so unbelievably sexy.

Levering up on his elbow, he freed the clasp on the front of her lace bra, and the fabric fell away from her full breasts. He drew on one rosy nipple, suckling her, and her back arched off the bed. He switched to the other breast and slid his finger inside her. Her muscles spasmed hard around him while she cried out. Stroking, he drew it out for as long as he could, relishing every sweet shudder of her body. When she finally settled, he drew the lace thong down her legs and off.

Then he settled between her thighs.

Her dark eyes met his, her cheeks still flushed and her lips glistening. He couldn't resist kissing her as he edged his way inside her.

She felt incredible.

So amazing he fought the urge to sink into her over and over again. He didn't want to rush her while she was still adjusting. He breathed through the need. Waiting.

"You okay?" He stroked a hand through her hair, let his thumb play over the fullness of her mouth.

"Good." She nodded, moving her hips as if to test the fit. "Really good."

Her sexy swivel was nearly his undoing. With pleasure, he returned the favor, working his hips. Taking what she offered. She was generous. Uninhibited. Passionate.

And he wondered if he could ever get enough.

The thought pulled him up short for a moment, but he shoved it away from him fast, needing to focus on Nicole. On her needs. Her wants. Her gorgeous body.

He rolled her on top of him, watching her, learning what she liked and how she liked it. But too soon, he felt his own release, too strong to hold back anymore. Reaching between them, he teased a touch over her. Once. Twice.

She stilled the third time, her body arching hard against him before she came with a soft, sweet cry. He let himself follow her, his shout drowning out hers until he was pretty sure he forgot his own name for a little while.

His breath rushed out in harsh pants, everything in him drained. Rolling to his side, he skimmed a hand through her hair.

Replete for the moment, he held her in his arms. He pulled the duvet over them to keep her warm, hoping what they'd just done didn't sabotage the working relationship they needed to have if they were going to find out the truth about her nephew.

About Zach.

At the thought, the temperature in the room dropped a few more degrees. A pit opened in his stomach. If Zach proved to be the father of Nicole's nephew, Desmond would want to maintain some kind of relationship with her in order to ensure the boy had everything he needed. What if he'd just impaired his chances of doing so by acting on the attraction? He stilled, the first shadow of guilt creeping over him. He couldn't afford to alienate Nicole. But hell, he couldn't afford to let her think this thing between them was more than—

"Don't go there," Nicole said quietly, stirring beside him. "Whatever you're thinking right now… don't. Don't worry about it."

He realized she'd been watching him. And damn it, he was usually better at concealing his thoughts. Regret for whatever she'd seen reflected in his face made him want to fix it. He cleared his throat and tried to pull his thoughts together.

"I was only thinking we should—"

She covered his lips with her fingers.

"We should eat." She sat up, releasing his mouth to clutch the duvet to her chest as she went. "Shouldn't we?"

Clearly, she didn't want to have a discussion about what had just happened.

He wished they'd met under any other circumstances so that they could not think about the consequences and simply enjoy each other over and over through the night. But he steeled himself, knowing that wasn't an option.

"Or we could discuss the monumental shift that just happened when we need to work together this week," he reminded her dryly. He switched on a small lamp near the bed, the low-wattage bulb still making him blink. "It's bound to change the dynamics between us."

She closed her eyes for a moment. When she reopened them, she met his gaze head-on. "Food first. Awkward conversation second. I'm too hungry to tackle uncomfortable subjects."

Was it wrong to table the discussion? But he understood about distracting hungers all too well. Or maybe he was ready for any excuse to delay talking about the inevitable—about why this attraction between them could never go any further.

She hurried to pull on her clothes again, and knowing she probably was battling possible regrets, he tried not to enjoy the view.

Tried.

When she was done, he pushed himself out of bed, guessing by her hasty retreat that he wasn't going to talk her into spending the night with him. Repeating what had just happened a few more times before dawn broke. Which was as it should be, no matter how much he wished otherwise.

He understood her distress. He couldn't deny having some of his own based on the difficult quest they needed to undertake together. As long as they both understood whatever was happening between them was temporary, they'd be fine. Because regretting what had just happened was impossible when he was already craving the chance to be with her again.

Nicole guessed the food was good, but she barely tasted anything in the aftermath of what had just happened in that bed. The incredible sex had been a revelation. The aftermath? She'd never forget the dark clouds that had filled Desmond's eyes afterward. She didn't know what he'd been thinking, exactly, but it had obviously been some form of "I've made a huge mistake" based on the furrow that had deepened between his eyes. The haunted expression in his gaze.

But for now, she could regroup while they ate.

Thankfully, Desmond had served them both, unwrapping dishes so she could expend her mental energies on pulling her thoughts back together. They sat side by side at counter stools in front of the narrow bar separating the tree house's living area from the small kitchen. Desmond, in deference to her wish to delay the inevitable discussion of what had just happened, made small talk about the ranch and its eco-friendly mission.

Nicole, in the meantime, absently stacked apple slices on her plate while wondering how to recover her footing in this relationship. She'd never experienced anything like what she and Desmond had shared. The intimate encounters that she'd had in the past had either been awkward or mildly enjoyable. There hadn't been anything close to urgent need, insatiable passion or a chemistry so potent it stole her breath. That she should feel all those things with Desmond, a man she had no reason to trust and every reason to be wary of, was unaccountable.

The situation made zero practical sense. She'd never thought of herself as the kind of woman who could just…combust like that. She could only attribute it to the stress she'd been under these last months since her sister's death. Her own grief had shaken her to her core. But her father had been—remained—inconsolable, and Matthew had needed a parent. So there hadn't been time to deal with her grief—she'd just had to push through.

Could that suppressed stress account for her over-the-top reaction to Desmond? Still too aware of him beside her, she considered the possibility while staring out a window at the graceful limbs of the maple trees that braced the cabin in the sky.

"Desmond." She interrupted his polite observations about the wildlife resurgence around Mesa Falls, needing to get the worst of the awkward conversation over. "I know that what happened today can't happen again." She congratulated herself for how steady her voice sounded despite the anxiety on the inside. "You don't have to worry that I'll have the wrong impression."

"It's not that I don't want it to happen again. Hell, if it was up to me, we'd—" His gray gaze roamed over her in a way that turned up the heat all over again. But he seemed to call back whatever he was going to say with an effort, shuttering the hunger in his eyes. "I just didn't want to give you the wrong idea about what it meant."

The hurt of that particular phrasing was sharp. And it pierced her far deeper than it should have. But she nodded, hoping he hadn't seen her flinch.

"I won't misunderstand," she assured him. Then, with an effort, she steered the conversation away from that land mine of them sleeping together. "Can I ask you a question about something unrelated?"

Hoping she appeared unaffected, she picked up a knife to spread a mild goat cheese onto a baguette slice. If she wanted any hope of redirecting her thoughts from their combustible chemistry and the emotional fallout of the aftermath, she needed to think of something besides how his touch had elicited the hottest moments of her life.

"Of course." He watched her, his gaze as sharp as ever.

"Earlier, when we were in the barn with the horses, you mentioned that Mesa Falls was built as a way to remember your friend Zach." At the time, she'd been too indignant at the prospect of the Mesa Falls partners flexing their financial weight to increase their say over Matthew's life to really look beyond the surface of the comment.

"What of it?" Desmond pushed back from the counter in his chair, his green Henley still lightly wrinkled where she'd fisted the fabric to draw him closer.

The memory of how he'd made her feel warmed her skin all over, although the realization that it couldn't happen again cooled her off again.

"Why Mesa Falls?" she asked in a rush, needing to return to her real reason for being here—unraveling the mystery of Matthew's father. "Did Zach like Montana? I'm just wondering why you chose this place when you all went to school in California."

Desmond refilled his water glass from the bottle before he answered.

"Two reasons. First, Zach liked Thoreau's book about life in the woods, and he talked about doing something like that. Getting a remote cabin and living away from everyone for a while." The words were so halting that she wondered if it was still hard for him to talk about his friend. "And also because he loved horses. The last trip we all took together, we were on horseback."

Nicole tried to remember what he'd told her about

his friend's death. When Desmond mentioned Zach the first time, she'd been preoccupied with the potential connection to Mattie. "He died in a cliff-jumping accident?"

A quick flash of emotion darted through his eyes before it was gone again. This time she didn't question if talking about his friend hurt, because clearly it did. But then, she knew she'd never get over the hole left in her since Lana's passing.

"Zach died during that last horseback riding trip. He jumped into a river from a well-known local spot. But it had rained the night before, and the water level was too high." Desmond stared without seeing, lost in a memory. "He'd been upset that weekend, but we didn't know why. He had a rough past, so we all assumed it had something to do with that."

An awful thought occurred to her. "You don't think he could have been upset because—"

"Because he'd just found out Lana was pregnant?" Desmond shook his head, not in denial so much as despair. "Believe me, I've been weighing that possibility myself. No doubt it would be upsetting news for any teenager, especially if it meant an illicit relationship with a teacher was going to come to light."

Her appetite fled, and she shoved aside her plate. "It can't have happened like that. If Zach jumped to his death right after Lana informed him of the pregnancy, she would have been devastated. She never would have been able to keep the news to herself—"

"She wouldn't have known." Desmond sounded

so sure of that point. "I didn't remember when she'd left teaching, but you said it was over Thanksgiving Break. That was the same time Zach died. And Dowdon kept the news of his death out of the papers for weeks. Even then, it was only a death notice with no reference to the school."

"She moved to Oregon. She probably wouldn't have seen it anyhow." Her belly knotted at the thought of her sister's affair. She'd always assumed Lana's boyfriend had rejected her, but if Zach was Matthew's father, the circumstances had been so much different than she'd imagined. It would make sense that Lana never admitted what had happened. "I'm surprised she wouldn't have tried getting in touch with him after Matthew was born. Or maybe she did…"

She trailed off, trying to recreate what could have happened. Feeling like she'd never known Lana at all. How would Matthew feel to learn something like this about his mother—that she'd had an affair with a student? "We're only just guessing that Zach knew about the pregnancy. She also could have broken things off with him without telling him about the baby, to protect them both from scandal. A breakup could also account for why he was upset that weekend." His jaw flexed as he began to wrap up the leftover food and clear the dishes they'd used.

She couldn't deny that sounded plausible. "Possibly. Maybe finding out she was pregnant made her come to her senses about what she was doing. She had to know that kind of relationship was wholly inappropriate. Not to mention illegal."

"If it even happened," he reminded her, tucking the food back into the insulated bag. "That's another big *if*, since we still can't be sure Zach is Mattie's father."

The frustration of the unanswered questions was evident in his voice. For the first time, Nicole began to see why Desmond needed to uncover the truth about Matthew's father, too. Clearly, Lana's pregnancy had significant implications for someone he'd cared about.

"Maybe meeting with your friends in a couple of hours will help." She found herself wanting to reassure him even though she had a lot of worries of her own.

She told herself that was just natural human empathy, but as they packed for the trip back to the ranch, she couldn't help but wonder if her need to comfort Desmond was part of the emotional fallout of getting close to him today.

"I hope so." His words were brusque, and something about his tone told her the subject was closed as he hefted the bag on his shoulder and passed her her jacket. "But before we go to dinner, I just want you to know that *I've* never believed Zach jumped to end his life."

Sliding her arms into the outerwear, Nicole followed him from the tree house. Any relief that she might have felt over avoiding an awkward conversation about where they stood since sleeping together was mitigated by the troubling new information about Zach Eldridge and her sister.

She'd almost reached the door when a small framed photo near the exit caught her eye. She hadn't noticed it on their way in.

"Desmond?" The image stopped her in her tracks. She reached up to trace the wavy line of a horse's mane behind protective glass.

Ahead of her, he stepped back into the tree house, sealing off the blast of cold air from outside.

"What's this?" Wary excitement teased the back of her brain, even though she wasn't sure what it meant. "Where did you get this?"

"It's one of Zach's sketches." He stood shoulder to shoulder with her, his nearness stirring her. "If it looks familiar, it might be because Alec Jacobsen, one of our partners, uses a stylized version in a popular video game he designed—"

He stopped himself, probably because she was already shaking her head.

"I have almost this same exact sketch at home." She'd never played a video game in her life, so she hadn't seen it there. "It belonged to my sister."

Seven

"You look like you could use a drink, mate," Gage Striker observed as he refilled Desmond's tumbler.

A drink? Desmond seriously doubted chugging the whole decanter of their host's best bourbon would take the edge off this evening. He'd brought Nicole to Miles Rivera's house for dinner with a few of his partners and their significant others. In theory, it should have been less tense than the last few meetings of the Mesa Falls partners since it was more of a social occasion. There had been less media focus on the ranch in the weeks since Vivian Stephens's arrest, plus the public was content with the explanation about Alonzo Salazar's book profits going toward humanitarian efforts.

Tonight, no one was looking over their shoulders, so they could relax. Jonah Norlander was back in Tahoe with his wife and daughter. Alec Jacobsen was globetrotting to promote one of his new games. But the rest of them were here. Dinner had been pleasant enough while they'd been making small talk. Gage's fiancée, Elena Rollins, had made a visible effort to put Nicole at ease, comparing notes with her about some of the more remote areas of Southern California they'd both visited.

Desmond had been intrigued to learn more about the redheaded bombshell who'd rocked his world only a few hours before, but he'd been forced to quit eavesdropping at that point to respond to something one of his partners had asked. Now, the group had relocated to the billiards room downstairs. The younger of the Rivera brothers—Weston—had challenged Miles to a round of eight-ball. Desmond sat at the sleek mahogany bar behind the game table while the four women made themselves comfortable on the leather sectional that wrapped the opposite corner of the room.

From his vantage point at the bar, Desmond could see Nicole peering at something Chiara Campagna showed her on her phone. A red wave slid forward over Nicole's shoulder as she leaned forward, her simple emerald-colored sheath dress hugging her curves the way he wanted to. Lost in thought about the dress and—damn—the curves, it took him a minute to register Gage's snicker from the bar stool near him.

"I'll take that as a 'Yes, I'll have a double.'" Accordingly, his hulking New Zealander friend splashed more bourbon into Desmond's tumbler before returning the decanter to the tray on the bar. "Care to explain why you can't tear your eyes away from our guest long enough to form coherent sentences?"

Desmond's response was a string of very coherent expletives that only increased Gage's amusement. Miles turned up the volume on the surround-sound speakers playing country music while Weston took the opening break and called his first shot.

Gage tucked a boot heel around the footrest of his bar stool as he straightened in his seat. "Hey, I'm only pointing out what's obvious to all your friends. Something's going on between you and Nicole Cruz, and it's more than just the mystery of her sister's son. The weird vibe was there from the moment you two entered the house before dinner." Gage lowered his voice as he raised his glass in front of his lips like a shield. "And when I say weird vibe, I mean the attraction is evident, so don't bother to deny it."

An attraction he'd stupidly shut down too fast by letting Nicole glimpse his doubts. He regretted that his need to define the relationship—to make it clear she couldn't expect more from him—had prevented them from enjoying each other again since that first time.

"Should I blame your engagement for this sudden intuitiveness? Or have you always been this full of sensitivity?" Desmond unbuttoned his suit jacket as he leaned an elbow on the bar, their seats swiveled to watch the pool game. Weston was on a run, calling his third shot. "And when I say *sensitivity*, I mean you're full of—"

"Skip the protests," Gage cut him off. The ice cubes clinked in his glass as he shook it lightly. "You know as well as I do you lose objectivity that way. I just finished walking that fine line myself, and I can tell you I'm glad to have come out on the other side of it."

Desmond couldn't question his friend's insight, not after what he'd been through. Gage and Elena had been estranged after a bitter separation six years prior, due to Gage's father's interference. When Elena had come to Mesa Falls for a scoop on the notoriously reclusive owners about the Hollywood tell-all book linked to their ranch, she'd not only been looking for a way to pay her bills. She'd also been ready to throw Gage under the bus because of their unhappy past. But the mutual attraction had undermined the efforts, leading them to renew their former engagement.

The whole scenario had been over-the-top. And lightning didn't strike twice in the same place. Although, looking around the room, where financial investigator April Stephens's eyes tracked Weston as he played pool, and social media influencer Chiara

Campagna sent a cheeky wink to Miles, Desmond amended that thought. Some Bermuda triangle kind of electrical storm must be hitting the Montana ranch to make three of his closest friends lose their heads over women in the last few months.

But he'd be damned if he'd follow their example.

"I'm not losing objectivity," Desmond countered, tossing back half of his bourbon in the hope it would give him enough patience for this conversation. "If things seem strained between Nicole and me, it's because we spend our time together talking about the past. About Zach."

Which was partially true. Her revelation about one of Zach's pictures belonging to her sister had circled around Desmond's head every bit as often as memories of being with Nicole. She'd taken a photo of the framed sketch in the tree house and planned to share it with the group, starting with Chiara, who knew the most about Zach's art. In fact, seeing the way Nicole pulled her phone from her narrow leather clutch, he guessed she was about to do just that.

Gage clapped a hand down on his shoulder. A brief, tangible commiseration. "No doubt, the memories can be rough. I'm hoping maybe, once we get through this mess and have more answers about the past, we can put the bad parts behind us for good. Focus only on what Zach gave us."

Desmond lifted his bourbon glass in silent toast to that idea.

"I hope." He took one more sip and then set the

tumbler aside, needing to be clearheaded to get through this evening. After the dinner party, he'd be driving Nicole back to the main lodge. Just the two of them. And he couldn't afford to make any more decisions based on the chemistry between them. "There was a time we thought Mesa Falls was going to do that—put the past to rest so we could focus on the good memories we all have of Zach."

"Alonzo Salazar's book being linked to Matthew Cruz made that impossible," Gage reminded him. "What remains to be seen is whether or not Matthew is Zach's son."

"And if he is, what role do we play as Zach's friends?" Nicole hadn't wanted to hear about the possibility of Matthew being deeded a portion of the ranch, but he knew his friends would insist on it.

Hell, *he'd* insist on it.

But he couldn't help a competing desire for Nicole's happiness, too. And it bugged him to think that she would be upset about him and his partners being more involved in Matthew's life. Just because he had no desire to be a parent himself didn't mean he'd jeopardize Matthew's future. Far from it.

He watched as Chiara took Nicole's phone from her, clearly engrossed in whatever Nicole showed her. The other women leaned closer to peer at the screen over Chiara's shoulder.

Nicole looked on, a tiny furrow between her auburn brows that made him want to kiss the spot to ease whatever worry put it there. And where the hell were thoughts like that coming from? He had thought—hoped—maybe acting on the heat between them would excise the tension between them. But if anything, taking her to bed had only added fuel to the fire, forcing him to acknowledge his fascination with her wasn't going away anytime soon. No matter that he'd made it clear things could never move beyond the physical.

He wanted her with a hunger—a fierceness—that backhanded him. The thought was interrupted when Chiara rose to her feet, Nicole's phone still in her hand.

"Gentlemen." Chiara stepped up to the billiards table, her floor-length gold gown making her look like she'd just stepped out of her own Instagram. But although she was one of the most photographed women in the world, her looks didn't compare to the redhead in emerald still seated on the love seat. At least, not in Desmond's eyes.

Miles put down his cue stick as she neared him. "What is it?"

"You all need to see this," Chiara announced before glancing back to where Nicole sat. "Right, Nicole? It's okay to share?"

Nicole nodded, but that small worry line was still etched in her brow. Desmond fought the urge to cross the room and sit beside her. Tuck her under his arm. It didn't matter that he'd made it clear their relationship had to be temporary.

He slipped off the bar stool, needing to see whatever Chiara had indicated. Gage followed him, and soon all eight of them crowded around the pool table as Chiara laid Nicole's phone next to her own. Nicole remained on the opposite side of the table from him, though her gaze landed on his once before flitting away again.

On the green baize–covered surface, Nicole's screen was lit, displaying the image of Zach's framed drawing in the tree house.

"When Nicole recognized one of Zach's sketches in Desmond's tree house earlier," Chiara began, "she had her father photograph a similar one that had been in her sister's possession." Chiara swiped a finger over Nicole's phone screen, revealing a second image almost identical to the first, except there were more background details and shading around the central image of the horse. "I think we can all agree the artist must be the same, especially put in context of the time they were drawn. Nicole knows Lana framed the drawing to hang in her son's bedroom, so she had it in her possession before Matthew's birth."

There was a murmur through the group.

Desmond's gaze darted to Nicole's face, wondering if he'd see any hint of guilt for not sharing the information with him first. Impatience simmered along with irritation that she'd kept quiet.

Chiara hit the home key on her own phone, bringing the next screen to life with an image of the box for Alec Jacobsen's most popular video game—*Hooves of Thunder*. The game box featured the main equine character prominently, and no doubt there was a resemblance between Zach's drawing and the now-iconic figure.

"We knew about that, though," Miles reminded his girlfriend, slipping an arm around Chiara's waist. He spoke gently, but somehow the tone brooked no argument. "And Alec gives Zach credit in the game."

"Right," Chiara acknowledged. "Posthumous credit for one character." She tapped Nicole's screen to brighten it once again and then swiped to change the image. A fox, a boar and a rooster appeared in quick succession, each one taking up a page in a sketchbook. "What about all these?"

Desmond sucked in a breath even before she tapped the second screen and swiped through those same characters as they appeared in screenshots from the popular video game. The resemblance was marked. Obvious.

Weston swore under his breath. Gage leaned closer to the table, blocking Desmond's view.

Instead, he looked to Nicole to gauge her expression, wondering if she'd made those connections. But her dark eyes were shuttered, leaving him to keep on wondering.

"What's the source of the sketchbook images?" Desmond asked, his attention still on Nicole.

She seemed to become aware of being everyone's focus, and she folded her arms around herself. Her chin lifted as she answered him. "I found a sketch-book in Lana's things when I cleared out her apartment. I boxed it up along with a few other important items because I recognized the style from the framed image she'd hung in Mattie's nursery."

Miles reached for Nicole's phone, stretching one of the images and scanning the borders of the paper. "None of the drawings are signed?"

Nicole's dark gaze shifted toward Miles. "No. My dad made a special trip to my house to photograph these things, and I asked him if he'd ship them all here tomorrow so you can examine them for yourselves."

The tension in the room was palpable, and not just because of the awkwardness between him and Nicole. Meaningful looks passed between all of the couples. A new uneasiness crept through Desmond.

He shared it with the group because it had to be on everyone's mind. "We're going to have to discuss what it means for us—for Mesa Falls—if Matthew Cruz is Zach's heir."

That didn't mean he wanted to have that discussion now, in front of Nicole. But they needed to acknowledge the likelihood. Prepare for it. Alec and Jonah would need to be roped in for a conference call since they weren't on-site.

Miles replaced the phone on the table. Nicole recaptured the device, squeezing the cover in a tight grip.

When she spoke, her tone was knife's-edge sharp. "Will you discuss what it means if your friend stole Zach's intellectual property? Or are you going to sweep that under the rug the way you've conspired to cover up Zach's whole existence?"

No doubt the accusation insulted every man in the room. But to Desmond, it sure felt heaped on him.

"That's not fair," he began, but she didn't seem interested in the explanation, because she swept up her leather clutch from the arm of the sofa and walked out of the room.

A few minutes later, Nicole stood alone in the front foyer of Miles Rivera's huge house on the ranch property, staring out the floor-to-ceiling windows onto the horseshoe-shaped driveway illuminated solely by landscape lights. She heard someone coming up the stairs from the billiards room and tensed.

She wasn't ready to talk to Desmond.

But the light tap of high heels on the tile floor made her turn around.

Chiara Campagna strode toward her, so beautiful she looked like her own personal filter followed her around at all times. With her perfect skin, rosebud lips and sheet of long, dark hair, she had fairy-tale princess beauty. Add in the flawless fit of her gold gown, the tasteful—and no doubt hugely expensive—accessories like the red-bottom shoes, sapphire cocktail ring and a bag by one of France's most coveted designers, and it was easy to see why the woman turned heads everywhere she went. And why her Instagram following rivaled the biggest celebrities in the world. Nicole couldn't help feeling underdressed by comparison.

Even so, Chiara and all of the other women at the small dinner party had welcomed her warmly. Chiara in particular had shown real interest in Matthew, asking about his childhood and his school program, demonstrating an earnest desire to know more about the boy. By contrast, her kindness had brought into stark relief how little Desmond had wanted to know about Nicole's nephew. The realization had been the first of two unhappy epiphanies over the course of the evening.

The way Desmond and his friends had hidden their dead friend's life and achievements rather than celebrate them put into perspective why it had been so damned hard to learn more about Matthew's connection to Mesa Falls. It was beginning to become clear to her now, however. Who could doubt Zach Eldridge had fathered her sister's son?

As Chiara drew nearer, Nicole refocused her thoughts.

"I hope I didn't offend you with my remarks," Nicole offered with an apologetic smile. "You've been nothing but kind to me."

Chiara took Nicole's hand and squeezed it briefly before letting go. "On the contrary, you asked the same kind of hard questions I've been putting forward to Miles for weeks."

Perhaps she didn't conceal her surprise very well, because Chiara continued.

"Trust me, I want answers as much as you do about Zach." A flash of pain streaked through the woman's eyes before she blinked, and the hurt was gone again. "And I think Miles and his partners— Desmond included—all want that, too. But they're torn and confused about what their next move should be."

"Then why have they conspired to hide Zach's life from the world?" Nicole had never seen a reference to him, making her question how the group would welcome his son. "If Mesa Falls is really their way of honoring Zach, where is the plaque in the lobby? Why no mention of him in the mission statement? They say they care, but it's like he never existed."

Chiara leaned a shoulder on the pane of glass overlooking the front yard, her golden gown reflecting the glow from a wrought iron chandelier in the foyer. "I think not talking about him is a habit long engrained. At the time, Gage Striker's politically ambitious father intervened with the school administration to keep the news of the death out of the local papers, and Dowdon was only too happy to oblige. And since none of Zach's friends had professional grief counseling as teens, they did a patch job on the trauma and somehow limped along with it, paying homage to Zach with the ranch."

Nicole mulled that over, wanting to believe things could be easily resolved. She knew how difficult Lana's loss had been for her. What might it have been like if something had happened to her when she'd been a teenager? She remembered Desmond's words when he'd first told her about it.

The death of someone I thought of as a brother left me walking around in a fog of grief for the better part of a year.

"What do you think they'll do now? They can't possibly deny that one of their own has been profiting off Zach's talents." Nicole had been stunned to see the images Chiara pulled up on her phone from Alec Jacobsen's popular video game. The similarity to the drawings in the sketchbook were obvious.

Chiara's dark eyebrows furrowed. "What's the earliest date you remember seeing that sketchbook in your sister's possession?"

"The year Matthew was born. I saw it in one of Lana's drawers when I was babysitting Mattie." She'd made the trip to Oregon for a visit, and to help watch her nephew while her sister worked.

"Good. That means no one can suggest the sketches were drawn after Alec's game came out. Whoever drew those images—and I know for a fact it was Zach—was a huge contributor to the success of the video game series." Shadows flitted through the other woman's eyes. "But it might take some time for Desmond—for all of them—to come to terms with the idea that one of their own is a traitor."

"I just hope the news doesn't distract them from figuring out if Zachary Eldridge is Matthew's father. It seems significant to me that my sister hung one of his drawings in her baby's nursery, almost as if she wanted a connection to the boy's father there. Finding out the truth about Mattie's dad is my only reason for being here."

The sound of footsteps preceded a man's voice behind her.

"Nicole, are you ready to leave?"

Desmond stood just a few feet away. Close enough that he must have overheard at least some of their conversation. She'd been so engrossed, she hadn't heard his approach. His steely eyes were cool now. His expression remote.

No hint of earlier intimacies lingered.

Which was just as well, right? He'd wasted no time making sure she didn't "get the wrong idea" about what had happened between them.

She needed to focus on tracking down Mattie's father, not indulge in a hot affair. So it didn't matter what Desmond thought of her now. Although she couldn't deny a sense of loss at the memory of his arms wrapped around her just hours ago. His kiss. His touch.

She blinked past the desire.

"Very ready," she assured him, matching his coolness. "Let me just say my good-nights and we can go."

Turning from him, she reminded herself it was for the best they break things off now rather than run the risk of someone getting hurt later. But knowing what was best for her didn't make it any easier to distance herself from the most compelling man she'd ever met.

Eight

Desmond stared at the computer screen in his study, poring over the details of Zach's drawings from the sketchbook that Nicole said she'd found in her sister's things.

Desmond hadn't wanted to wait until the actual book arrived. He'd asked her to send him digital copies of the photo images after the dinner party at Miles's house. It had been the extent of their conversation on the ride home, since neither of them had been in the mood to talk.

Finding out the truth is the only reason I'm here, she'd told Chiara, referring to her search for Matthew's father. The simple statement shouldn't have been any surprise to him. He'd known as much. But considering what had transpired between the two of them—the desperate can't-get-enough-of-each-other sex—maybe Desmond had hoped that he'd ranked somewhere in her reasons to be in Montana.

Apparently not.

While he shoved that thought aside with the weariness of a man who'd done the same thing a hundred times, a knock sounded on his study door.

"Come in," he answered, never glancing up from the screen.

"Mr. Pierce?" A woman with his cleaning service opened the door a sliver. "A Miss Cruz is in the front room for you."

His stomach dropped like he'd just buckled into an amusement park ride. But he simply powered off the screen and stood.

"Thank you." He dismissed her with a nod. "I'll be right with her."

He told himself that whatever Nicole wanted didn't have a damned thing to do with him. No doubt she had more questions for him about Zach's past or the drawings, or some other connection between her nephew and Mesa Falls. But knowing as much didn't stop a jolt of hunger for more.

Much, much more.

As he closed the study door behind him, he wanted to believe that the need for her was purely physical. Their connection had been unlike anything he'd ever experienced before, the memories of it so hot and all-encompassing that thinking about her could drag him right back to that afternoon, enticing him to relive every minute of it over and over again. And something about that overwhelming sensual immersion made him fear what he felt for Nicole went beyond the physical. Her protectiveness for Matthew made her a force to be reckoned with, a job she'd undertaken even though she wasn't Lana's—or Matthew's—blood relation.

Desmond admired the hell out of that kind of loyalty, especially after growing up in the kind of household he had. Nicole's commitment to Matthew humbled him.

Nearing the formal living room at the front of the house, Desmond braced himself for the inevitable effect of seeing her. He'd thought his first glimpse of Nicole in her sleep camisole had been the reason for his fascination. But he now realized she could have been wearing layers of sweats and he still would have been every bit as captivated.

"Nicole." He spoke the name like he was releasing a breath, all the pent-up need for her appeased—in part, at least—by seeing her again.

Today, she wore a pale blue sweater with a gray wrap skirt, the hem printed with the image of an iris bloom. Her long auburn hair hung in loose waves around her shoulders, the ends spiraling in ringlets he wanted to coil around his fingers. Had she gone to extra effort for him, he wondered? The idea was appealing, but he dismissed it, recalling her words.

Finding out the truth is the only reason I'm here.

He'd do well to focus on that.

"I hope I didn't disturb you," she began, turning from the view of Trapper Peak and the Bitterroot Mountains. "I received the sketchbook by special delivery today. I thought it might help to see the physical object, since my father didn't photograph all of it."

She pointed toward a flat package he hadn't noticed propped against a table near the front door.

There was something detached in her manner today, the same reserve that had been there since they'd left Miles's house the night before. He should be grateful for it.

Instead, he could only think about how much he'd rather have her hands on him. Peeling off his shirt. Her fingernails pressing into his shoulders as he did something that pleased her. Yeah, he hated the distance between them.

"You didn't disturb me." He took another step toward her, as if pulled there by invisible force. "I was looking at the photo images of the sketches, so if anything, the arrival of the original makes the work easier."

The cover of the book hadn't been photographed, for instance. He wondered if there were clues to the owner's identity on the inside cover or on the back.

"What are you looking for in the drawings?" she asked, sounding a little breathless.

Because he was closer to her? He hoped so.

"I'm not entirely certain," he admitted, wishing he

had more concrete answers. "But finding something new of Zach's—something I didn't know existed before—is like hearing his voice again."

Her dark eyes tracked his. The fact that she looked up at him now made him realize he'd somehow moved closer still.

"I know what you mean." She nodded, the red curls dancing around her shoulders with the movement. "I spent a long time going through Lana's belongings after her death. Touching things she'd touched. Discovering little treasures that I knew must have been important to her based on where I found them. A note in a jewelry box drawer. A dried corsage from a long-ago dance."

A vulnerable look passed through her eyes, and he couldn't resist the urge to touch her. He stroked a hand over the silky length of her hair, sifting his fingers through the soft curls.

"I can't imagine how tough this year has been for you." He admired her grit for taking on all that she had. Loss of her sister aside, there would have been a lot of practical matters to take care of in securing legal guardianship of her nephew. "It couldn't have been easy to become a parent overnight."

For a moment, she stood very still. Not moving nearer, but not moving away, either. He fought the need to bend his lips to her hair and kiss the top of her head. To pull her against him fully and offer her the comfort of his arms around her.

But then she stepped back and out of his reach.

She returned to the window overlooking the mountains.

"It was awful." Her voice revealed the power of her emotions or he might have been more troubled by her need for space. She hugged her arms around her waist. "My father was devastated. He's still inconsolable about losing Lana. So I didn't have any help from him in comforting Matthew." She glanced back at him over her shoulder. "And Matthew processed his grief a little differently from how you might expect a boy his age would."

Desmond shook his head. "If I learned one thing from Zach's death, it's that people—all of us—process grief uniquely. Alonzo Salazar was good about finding us all outlets to deal with it."

"How did you deal with it?" she asked, surprising him.

He debated how much to say. He'd never been comfortable revealing that part of his life, but if he ever wanted the chance to be close to this woman again, he couldn't keep pulling away. He'd been the one to put the distance between them that he already regretted.

"Good works." He crossed the living area to stand near her at the window. "I put every second of my free time into helping at a local shelter that benefited battered women and kids. I needed to build something positive. It was my way of honoring a cause that was important to Zach."

Her dark eyes were perceptive.

"I remember how concerned you were when I mentioned Lana's father was abusive," she remarked softly. "Did Zach come from a violent home?"

"We both did." It was an admission he'd never made to a woman before. Only his friends knew about his past. "Zach was the first person to recognize what my home life was like. He—"

The memory of that bond—of finding someone who understood, someone he didn't have to explain to—the relief and gratitude he'd felt were beyond explanation to anyone who hadn't lived that particular hell. "He helped me get through it. To fight back."

She slid her fingers through his, a touch so welcome he couldn't help but squeeze her palm tight at the wordless support. The understanding all the more valuable because it wasn't tinged with pity.

Dragging in a long breath, he continued. "Anyway, I put all my grief into volunteering at the center. Sorting donated clothes, refereeing games for the little kids, cleaning the place. Whatever they needed. I organized a class fundraiser through Dowdon that helped the center purchase a new building."

"You were far more productive during your mourning than I've been during mine. Some days I feel like I'm barely hanging on." She stared down at their interlaced fingers. "When I let myself think about the fact that I'll never talk to her again, it hurts so much it's almost hard to breathe."

With his free arm, he pulled her against him, pinning their locked hands between their bodies. For a long moment, he simply held her, wishing he could take away some of the pain. Knowing there was no way to fast-forward through the steps of grieving a loss like that. He couldn't tell her that the loss got any easier, because in his experience, it didn't. You just got better at finding ways to deal with the pain of missing someone.

She stirred against him and he released her, sensing she might need to collect herself. She ran a hand through her hair, her long skirt swishing around her calves where high leather boots hugged her legs.

"I should show you the original sketchbook my father shipped to me," she murmured, half to herself, as she paced near the narrow package leaning against a table. "Chiara seems positive this book belonged to Zach. She didn't remember seeing him with this one in particular, but she pointed out a few doodles on the cover that he liked to make on all his books."

"Has she already seen the original?" Desmond moved to help Nicole lift the kraft paper–covered book onto the coffee table. He held the paper while she tugged the book free.

She dropped into the closest love seat, and he sat beside her. His knee grazed hers, the contact enough to send his thoughts hurtling back to the tree house, where he'd gotten intimately acquainted with every square inch of her. Their gazes collided, and he would bet from the way hers darted from his that she was remembering the same thing.

"No. But last night she texted me photos of some

ink drawings she made from memory. Then, when this arrived today, I sent her a picture of the cover." Nicole withdrew her phone from her leather handbag and turned the screen toward him. "These were her images."

Desmond took the device from her, carefully reviewing the ink sketches along with Chiara's note about the designs Zach liked to doodle while he was thinking. They were simple, repetitive patterns that were shaped into bigger designs. Feathers and scales, flower petals and leaves.

"Would you agree he drew that kind of thing?" Nicole asked, glancing at the phone.

The scent of her hair tempted him to lean closer, to bury his face in the softness of all that red silk.

"It looks sort of familiar, but I wouldn't be able to say for certain. Chiara would know, though. They attended an art camp together that summer, and from what I gather, she paid close attention to his work."

"She told me she had a huge crush on him." Nicole smiled. "I'm sure she hoarded every scrap of information about him that was available to her fifteen-year-old self." She slid the sketchbook toward him. "Now take a look at this."

Desmond set down the phone on the coffee table and took up the softbound book held shut with an elastic band. Artwork covered the formerly brown cover. A partial lion's face covered half, the elaborate mane consisting of all the variations of doodles Chiara had anticipated—feathers, scales, petals, leaves.

Each section of the mane was a little different, so that even though there might be four sets of feathers, each of them was decorated a different way, with broken lines or dots, squiggles or solid shading.

He traced the bisected lion's face with his finger, lost in thought. He remembered Zach drawing all the time. Between classes, during classes, even at night in their dorms when the rest of them were shoving, wrestling or otherwise hanging from the rafters. Hell, Zach had drawn while doing homework, one hand on his pencil, the other cueing up a video lecture. Desmond would have lost those memories without this reminder right in front of him. A tangible voice from the past that Nicole had given him.

She leaned closer, her hair spilling partially onto his shoulder as she looked at the book with him.

"The similarities can't just be coincidence," she observed quietly before peering into his face. "Can they?"

He knew she wanted him to confirm her suspicions. Give her some kind of proof that his dead friend was the father of her nephew. But as much as he wanted to help her solve the mystery, he couldn't be positive.

"I wish I had answers for you, Nicole. But we're trying to reconstruct the past with a patchwork of guesses. We've lost all of the people with the power to confirm or deny our suppositions."

She frowned, edging back to consider him. "You don't think this is your friend's sketchbook?"

"Actually, I do." The memories of Zach drawing returned to his brain. Clear. Crisp. Like they'd just been back at Dowdon the day before. "Not just because Chiara recalled the things he drew. But because of the sketches inside. The similarity to the horse in the tree house. The similarity to the images Alec used."

There were too many things that tied Zach to the book, including when it came into Lana Allen's possession.

"Then why did you hesitate?" She retrieved her phone, returning it to her purse.

Inserting space between them.

He knew he needed to let her go. They weren't going to end up in each other's arms again anytime soon, no matter how much he wanted that. Wanted her. But he couldn't help wishing he could rewind things, and…hell. He didn't know. He couldn't give her the answers she needed.

"Because even though I think this book belonged to Zach, it still doesn't seem like enough proof that Zach is Matthew's father. And bottom line, that's what you want to know."

She went very still. Then, stiffly, began to slide the sketchbook back into the packaging.

"Let me," he offered, taking over the task.

He tucked the corners of the paper cover around the book and then stood it on end beside the love seat.

"Has anyone reached out to Alec Jacobsen to ask

him about the images he used in his game?" As she rose to her feet, her skirt brushed his leg briefly.

The need to pull her back to him was so strong that he jammed his hands in the front pockets of his pants as he stood.

"We've tried." He hated to be the one to deliver the news, but she had a right to know. "He was supposed to be watching over things at the casino for me this week, but he hasn't been seen on-site since last night."

"What?" Tension radiated from her stiff shoulders. Her fists clenched at her sides. "Meaning he took off as soon as one of your friends tipped him off that we know he stole more of Zach's artwork than he gave him credit for."

She whirled away from him, skirt flaring.

"No." He hastened to place himself between her and the door. "There's no way that happened. I'm positive."

"Oh, really?" She halted just inches from him. Close enough to touch. "Last night was Miles's dinner party. Last night eight of us stood around a billiard table and saw evidence that suggests Alec Jacobsen is a thief. The timing is damning." Her breathing was hard. Fast.

He wished it was because they were almost touching. But anger sizzled off her words.

"No one tipped him off," he repeated, staring directly into her furious brown eyes.

"How do you know?" Her gaze narrowed.

She didn't back down.

And it was a good thing he'd kept his hands in his pockets, because the need to touch her still rode him.

"Because I employed the same private investigator that followed you to Prince Edward Island to keep an eye on Alec for us."

Did she trust him enough to believe him?

The misplaced awareness she felt for Desmond was short-circuiting her brain, making her unsure what to think. Falling into bed with him had shaken all her prior convictions like so many puzzle pieces, scattering them in every direction until she couldn't put them together anymore.

Recognizing the effect was all the stronger the closer she stood to him, she edged back a step. She needed a breath that wasn't tinged by the sandalwood scent of his aftershave.

"If you're having him watched, why don't you know where he is?" She crossed her arms. As if she could create a barrier between herself and the desire for the man standing between her and the exit.

Not that she wanted to leave now.

"I never said I didn't know where he is." His hands were still fisted in his pockets, his shoulders looking every bit as tense as hers felt right now. "I said no one has seen him at the casino, which he's supposed to be managing for me."

She arched an eyebrow. Waiting.

"He's in New York," Desmond continued. "I still

hope he's got a damned good reason to be there, but his movements make me think he could be planning to leave the country." His gray eyes scanned her, and he gestured toward the living room. "Will you sit back down, and we can discuss it?"

She wasn't sure she trusted herself to be that close to him again. The memories of their time together were never far from her mind. Seeing his hands move over the sketchbook earlier had brought her right back to those hot moments when his palms had wandered all over her naked body. Even now, she had to suppress a shiver.

"I'm fine here, thank you." She sounded terse. She couldn't help it. "What makes you think he's leaving the country?"

"The PI reported that Alec updated his passport. Also that he has an appointment with his financial adviser this afternoon."

"Why did you have him followed? Is it because you believe—like I do—that your friend profited from Zach's work without giving him any real credit?" She'd researched the game thoroughly before falling asleep last night. She'd even bought a copy to give to Matthew. "I read the credits on the box, by the way. Zach's name isn't there."

"I had him followed because I'm not entirely convinced Vivian Fraser would have acted alone to threaten Chiara, the way Alec's assistant claimed." He sounded troubled about that. "And for what it's worth, Alec acknowledged Zach's influence on his video game in a well-publicized video—"

"Anonymously. I saw the video." She couldn't help but feel indignant. She'd only just learned about Zach Eldridge, the young man who'd died too soon, but she felt defensive of him. "And I noticed how Alec protected himself from having to share any earnings with Zach's potential heir by never mentioning Zach's name."

Desmond watched her, the muscle in his jaw flexing. She hadn't made up her mind that Matthew was Zach's son, but she couldn't deny the evidence in favor of Zach as the father was strong. She knew for a fact that Lana and Zach had spent time together before she'd started working as a student teacher at his school. The fact that Lana had kept his artwork was telling, as was Zach's mentor offering anonymous support for the boy after Zach's death. Add to that the realization that Lana had left town distraught, at the same time Zach had gone on that horseback riding trip, also extremely upset, which strongly hinted at a falling-out between them.

When Desmond finally spoke, his words were slow. Deliberate. "I promise you, if Matthew is Zach's son, I will move heaven and earth to be sure he's well provided for."

Everything in Desmond's voice and his manner echoed his sincerity. But the commitment brought her back to another fear that had never gone away since she'd set foot in Montana. Would the powerful men of Mesa Falls use their influence to somehow supplant her in Matthew's life?

"Thank you." She appreciated his promise, the first and only time anyone had offered her tangible help in her sudden role as a parent. "I'm grateful for that. Just as long as you agree to recognize my rights as his acting parent."

The small smile he gave her was a sad one. "Of course. After my childhood, I have no aspirations to fatherhood, believe me."

They spoke a little longer about the next steps in potentially proving Matthew was Zach's child. Nicole would contact the California Department of Social Services to request information about Zach's relatives in order to obtain a DNA sample that would legally prove paternity. Desmond agreed to retain a lawyer to help her with a claim since Alec's gaming empire was worth a fortune, an expense Desmond insisted on bearing since Zach was his friend. But by the time she left his house to show the sketchbook to Chiara, the only thing on her mind was Desmond's assurance that he would never be a father.

It shouldn't be any of her business.

Yet telling herself that didn't ease the hurt she felt for him and the painful past he'd admitted. She'd be willing to bet he didn't share that part of himself easily. Or often.

Having him trust her with that part of himself

made her feel closer, more connected to him. Although knowing that he wanted no part of family life put him farther out of her reach than ever.

Nine

Nicole met Chiara and Elena at Gage's house on the Mesa Falls property.

The women gathered around a table in Elena's studio, a workspace in progress that Gage had helped design for her new career in fashion design. Dark hardwood floors and neutral walls scaled up to the cathedral ceilings, broken only by tall windows and a huge skylight to increase the natural light. Architectural salvage pieces—old doors and window frames of various sizes—stood against one wall waiting to be incorporated into the room. The only finished section was a reading nook with a faux-fur chaise lounge surrounded by built-in bookshelves.

While Elena and Chiara flipped through the

sketchbook, Nicole admired the aesthetic of the work space, along with the obvious care and thought that went behind it. Her home office amounted to a corner of her living room where she'd stationed a consignment-shop table to hold her laptop and her drawing supplies for when she wanted to create by hand. How much more productive might she be with this kind of inspiration and room to work? She was busy imagining where she'd place an easel to paint when Chiara's voice interrupted her thoughts.

"There's not a single doubt in my mind that this is Zach's sketchbook," the social media star announced after she'd been reviewing the book for about ten minutes. Her long dark hair pooled on the table as she bent over the pages. "And every one of Alec's trademarked game characters is in here—years before his game came out. So if you prove that Zach is Matthew's father, you'll also have legal grounds for suing Alec for stealing intellectual property from Zach's heir. If you end up needing me to testify that this is Zach's work, I will do so gladly."

That all sounded so far in the future given that she hadn't even confirmed Zach was her nephew's father yet. But she was touched that Chiara was willing to go on record about the creator of the sketches. Desmond would be hiring an attorney for her paternity claim, and Nicole had already contacted Social Services in between her stop at Desmond's place and Gage's.

"I appreciate that." Nicole joined them at the table

where a stylized sketch of an owl in flight filled the page. "Do you mind sharing what makes you so certain that this is Zach's work?"

In the pocket of her skirt her phone vibrated, but she ignored it to focus on whatever Chiara had discovered.

"His name on the cover, for one thing." Chiara flipped to the front of the sketchbook, her black-and-white-striped nail art a contrast with the simple brown cover.

"But there's no handwriting anywhere." Frowning, Nicole scanned the few doodles around the bottom edge, searching for hidden letters.

"See these dots and dashes?" Chiara ran her index finger along the top edge of a geometric border drawn in shaded triangles.

"Morse code," Elena announced, spinning the book so she had a better angle on the pattern of dots and dashes. "My father taught it to me when we were camping in the desert, only we used a flashlight to communicate with it—pulsing the light on and off."

"Seriously?" Nicole wondered if she could have missed it in other drawings. The possibility made her want to review all the other sketches more carefully. "How did you know Zach used that?"

Her phone vibrated again, and she squeezed it to shut off notifications for now.

"He liked the idea of incorporating letters and symbols into graphic patterns." Chiara sketched a squiggle on a piece of notebook paper nearby while she spoke. "He showed me some things he wrote with Chinese characters and Sanskrit the summer we took an art class together. And once, he used Morse code in the scales of a snake he painted. Sort of like this." She twisted her sketch toward Nicole so she could see the lines on the snake's back were actually a series of dots and dashes.

While Nicole's gaze went from the note paper to the sketchbook, Elena brought up the Morse code alphabet on her phone.

"Look at this." Elena held it above the cover of Zach's collected sketches. "Here's the Z. Two dashes and two dots."

Excitement knotted up with apprehension at the chance of confirming the identity of Matthew's father. The notebook didn't prove it, of course, but it was one more piece of evidence that underscored the importance of Lana's relationship with Zach. She'd kept his drawings all her life, and carefully framed one of them to hang in Matthew's nursery. The picture remained in the boy's room even now. Proving for certain who fathered her nephew would be a huge worry relieved. And while Nicole regretted that Matthew would never have the chance to get to know his dad, at least his father wouldn't be a giant question mark in the boy's mind. Zach's friends all mourned him deeply. That said a lot about his character.

After everything Desmond had confided about his friend, Nicole couldn't imagine Zach had been consumed by despair when he'd jumped into the river that day. His death was an accident. Desmond believed that. And she trusted his instincts.

About that, at least. She wasn't so sure about his instincts where she was concerned. Seeing him just now had stirred up the attraction and—if she was being honest—feelings, too. She closed her eyes briefly to block out those thoughts and focus on why she was here. Finding answers about her nephew so she could return home.

"Mattie will enjoy the puzzle of the Morse code," Nicole remarked aloud, recalling the way his mind worked. "He'll think that's very cool when I show him the sketchbook." Then, another thought occurred to her as she addressed Chiara. "Did Zach ever mention being on the spectrum?"

"Not to me. And if Miles or any of his friends had thought so, I'm sure they would have mentioned it once they knew about your nephew." Chiara straightened from the table and stretched her arms over her head as if to work out a kink in her back from bending. "But if you can prove paternity, the Department of Social Services will have to share any medical records relevant to Matthew's health. They might be able to tell you if Zach was ever tested."

"At least I know they shared one trait in common." Nicole withdrew her phone to check her messages. "Matthew is artistic, too. He loves to draw."

Glancing down at her device, she saw the calls had been from Desmond.

"Does he really?" Chiara asked, her gaze as warm

and inviting as her tone. "I hope we get to meet him one day. Whatever happens with the paternity case, Nicole, he already feels like Zach's family to me."

The kindness in the sentiment tugged at her, distracting her from whatever reason Desmond had phoned her. She wanted more of a sense of family for Matthew. He'd grown up without a father, and now his mother was gone, too. His grandfather—who'd always been close to him—was still reeling from losing his daughter. How nice would it be to introduce Matthew to someone like Chiara, who'd known the man who was, in all likelihood, his father. To hear stories about his father from someone who'd known him. Like Chiara.

Also like Desmond, a troublemaking portion of her brain insisted on reminding her. But just because Matthew would like Desmond didn't mean she should introduce them. Desmond had made it clear he wasn't interested in children. And even if he might be interested in a boy who wasn't his child, that didn't make him a good bet for being around a teen who needed stable, consistent figures in his life.

But before Nicole could tell Chiara how much her kindness meant to her, a sharp rap sounded on the door to Elena's workspace.

"Elena?" Gage stood in the open door, his knock apparently more of a courtesy than a formality as he stepped just over the threshold. "Sorry to interrupt, love, but I thought you should know I just heard from Desmond." The New Zealander's gaze shifted to Nicole. "He tried to reach you first, Nicole. He wanted you to know he received a message from Vivian Fraser's attorney."

Chiara drew in a sharp breath. "That's Alec's assistant," she reminded Nicole. "The one who hacked my social media and tried to silence me in my search for answers about Zach."

Nicole recalled all too well why Desmond had Alec followed. He didn't believe Vivian acted alone. "What did she want?"

Gage walked deeper into the room, looping an arm around Elena's shoulders as he spoke. "Vivian claims she has new information about both Alec and Zach, but she won't talk to police unless Matthew Cruz's guardian is present."

Uneasy, Nicole went still, unsure what her next move should be. Could the woman know the relationship between Zach and Matthew when no one else had? Or had Alec known all along and purposely kept it hidden to deny Matthew his rights and potential inheritance as Zach's heir? "Maybe Vivian isn't pleased her former lover is leaving the country without her. Perhaps she's ready to share more about his scheme to deny Matthew the legacy and inheritance that should have belonged to his father."

Chiara asked, "Is Vivian still being held in Tahoe?"

"Yes." Gage tucked Elena even closer as he spoke, a swirl of dark tattoos around his wrist visible as his shirtsleeve rode higher on his arm. "Nicole, Desmond said he already called our pilot. If you want to meet with Vivian, Desmond dispatched a car to pick you up here and take you to the airport."

His words broke through her uncertainty, reminding her of her only objective in Montana—to find Matthew's father. If that meant leaving Mesa Falls, she would. With or without Desmond. And since Desmond had made no mention of joining her, she couldn't imagine that he would. Which made sense since it was her quest, not his.

Although she couldn't deny a spike of envy for the obvious support a couple like Gage and Elena were able to give to one another. Seeing the comfort they took just from touching triggered a whole host of memories and emotions for what she'd shared with Desmond.

It hadn't been the same, of course. Desmond had made it clear that their time together had been an isolated incident. Something they didn't carry back into their day-to-day lives. In theory, she appreciated that. But since then, she couldn't deny she'd thought of him often. Wondered about the possibility of being with him that way again.

Realizing the others stood around her, no doubt waiting for her reaction, Nicole scooped up the sketchbook.

"I need to find out what she knows," she murmured, tucking the book under her arm. "Thank you for everything. Your welcome and support mean a lot to me."

Elena stepped forward to wrap her in a quick hug. "Good luck, Nicole. Let us know if we can help."

Touched, Nicole hugged her back, letting Elena's lavender fragrance and good wishes surround her. "Thank you."

No sooner had Elena stepped back than Chiara followed suit, hugging Nicole. "You'll be back here soon with Matthew, I hope," Chiara reminded her. "Or I'll come to you if that's easier. I can't wait to meet him."

Nicole thanked her, too, and let Gage accompany her to his front door. Outside, a car was already waiting for her, a uniformed driver standing in the driveway near the rear of the sleek black SUV with heavily tinted windows.

She would text Desmond once she was inside to let him know she'd received his message and would gladly accept his offer of the flight to Tahoe. Although maybe a little part of her was hurt that he was so efficiently facilitating her speedy exit from Mesa Falls. Was he so eager for her to be out of his life? A tender part of her heart resented that he didn't want the complications of a child. What use would she have ever had for a man without room for Mattie in his heart?

Indignant, she greeted the driver with a nod as he opened the rear door of the SUV while a cold wind whipped off the nearby mountains.

She stepped up into the warm interior, the scent of expensive leather tickling her nose as she took her seat and withdrew her phone to text Desmond. The door shut behind her at the same time the front partition window lowered with an electronic hum.

Glancing up at the sound, she realized two things simultaneously. First, that the driver was still outside the vehicle swiping snow from the hood.

Second, that Desmond sat in the passenger seat. The sight of him seemed to flip an invisible switch inside her, lighting up all her nerve endings.

He held his phone in one hand as he pivoted to look at her over one broad shoulder.

"I'm finishing up some business before the flight and didn't want to bother you if you had your own calls to make. Do you want to stop at the main lodge before we take off?" He must have told his caller to hold, as he directed all his attention to Nicole while he waited for her to answer.

She suppressed a shiver of awareness, resenting the tangible physical reaction she felt around him. Especially when her focus should be on this new development in her quest to find Mattie's father. But there was no denying Desmond's attentiveness— from arranging the flight to anticipating her desire to leave as soon as possible—stirred her as much as the thought that he planned to join her.

"Yes, please. I'd appreciate a stop at the lodge for my things." She cleared her throat to try and banish the smoky sound of her voice before she continued, "I take it you're…going to fly to Tahoe with me?"

"I have every intention of hearing what Vivian

has to say. I want answers as much as you do, Nicole." His gray eyes turned the molten silver shade she remembered from their time together. "Assuming you don't mind if I join you?"

She opened her lips to speak, but her mouth had gone dry at the idea of them spending more time together. Alone. She settled for a nod.

No doubt Desmond read her thoughts, because there was an answering heat in his gaze. But thankfully, their driver returned to put the SUV in gear and start their trip, allowing Nicole to hide her suddenly warm cheeks as she ducked to look at her phone.

Desmond gave Nicole space on the flight to Tahoe.

He'd purposely taken a seat on the opposite side of the aisle from her in the private jet. Although they were facing one another, they each had their own worktable to spread out their things during the flight. He'd sensed her confusion—and, yes, her reaction to him—in the car ride on the way to the airport. He didn't want to press her if she was feeling unsure about their time together. Hell, she wasn't alone in the confusion or the attraction.

Ever since the heat had overtaken them in the tree house, Desmond had questioned himself about letting things spiral out of control. But he was also very aware of her every time they were in the same room. And trying to ignore their chemistry was an exercise in futility. If anything, the distance he'd attempted to put between them had only intensified the draw. Or maybe it was intensified because now he knew what it was like to be with her.

In the seat opposite him, Nicole powered off her tablet and tucked it into its neoprene sleeve. When they'd stopped at the main lodge before the flight, she'd changed into a simple black knit dress with boots and a pale beige tweed blazer for travel. The rich color of her hair seemed all the more vibrant against the neutral colors.

"How much longer until we land?" she asked, running a finger under her gold watchband to adjust the position on her wrist.

He glanced at his phone before leaning back in his seat. "Less than thirty minutes."

"Do you have any guesses what Vivian could want?" She switched from fiddling with her watch to flipping the oval pendant she wore around her neck on a long gold chain. "Or why she's suddenly decided to reveal more than when she was first arrested?"

He fought the urge to reach across the table and cover her restless fingers. But then, maybe he was just looking for an excuse to touch her again.

"I reached out to her attorney to let him know that Alec was on the move, possibly to leave the country." It still galled him to think that a man he trusted— one of his closest friends—could have been working against their interests all this time. "I suggested he relay the information to his client in case she knew more about Alec's activities than what she'd admitted when she was first arrested."

Nicole's fingers paused in their twirling of the pendant.

"That was clever of you." A gleam of respect lit her dark brown gaze. "How well do you know her?"

"Not well at all. Which, in retrospect, I see must have been by design on Alec's part. Vivian attended Brookfield, the girls' school closest to Dowdon. He's known her that long, and yet he always kept her apart from us."

"So she wasn't just his employee. They were friends?"

"Yes. And lovers at times, apparently." Some of that had been covered in the news articles he'd forwarded to Nicole about Vivian's arrest. "Did you have the chance to read the press I sent you?"

"I did. Thank you." She tucked a red wave behind one ear and glanced out the window before lowering the shade a few inches to block the setting sun. "Just wondering your take on their relationship versus what the news outlets had to say."

"Alec has been focused on building a gaming empire. Personal relationships haven't been a priority for as long as I've known him." For him, either. Even when life had been less complicated.

"It sounds like you have that much in common with him." Her gaze slid briefly to his before darting away again.

He studied her for a long moment, not sure how

to respond. He folded down the table in front of him so he could switch seats to the one beside her. Heat flared in her eyes when he looked at her again.

Even though, damn it, that's not why he'd closed the distance between them. Was it?

"I may not have wanted personal relationships to be a priority in the past, but I'm rethinking that now." He let her mull that over while he did, too. Because the realization surprised him also, but that didn't make it any less true. He hadn't been able to stop thinking about her. And not just because of their heated connection. He wanted to help her. To know more about her. "Recently, I've started to remember what my mentor told me long ago about all work and no play."

His fingers lifted, as if by their own volition, and sifted into the cinnamon strands that framed her face. He combed through the tendrils slowly, watching them glide over his skin.

The only sound besides the rumble of the jet engine was Nicole's swift intake of breath.

A wash of color crept up her cheeks, flooding over the smattering of freckles. The need to kiss everywhere that flush landed was a sudden overwhelming need.

"I can't afford to play, Desmond." Her words were softly spoken, with little volume behind them, but they still delivered a gut punch to his midsection. "I'm the head of a family now. I need to make smart decisions."

"I have no doubt that you will. You've already championed your nephew to ensure his future is secure, and I admire that." His thumb traced her cheekbone, smoothing along impossibly soft skin. He would let her go in another moment. Once he was sure she really wanted to walk away. "But we still have a brief window of time together before our responsibilities claim us again. Would it be so wrong to indulge something we want? Something solely for ourselves?"

She closed her eyes for a moment, and he thought he'd lost any chance. Without opening them, she said, "When we land, we'll go see Vivian. Find out what she knows. And then I'll go resume my life while you resume yours." Her lashes fluttered open again, her look fixing him. "I thought that's what you wanted. You were adamant that I didn't get the wrong idea about what happened between us."

He'd had plenty of opportunities to curse those words he'd spoken. But the fact that he hadn't been able to organize his thoughts after being with her only underscored how much she'd gotten under his skin.

"I wanted to be honest with you. Then and now. I know I don't have anything to offer beyond tonight, but I won't pretend I don't still want you." So. Much. She was ever present in his thoughts. In his memories. In fevered dreams. "Visiting hours at the jail will be over when we land," he continued, hoping he wasn't deceiving himself that there could still be one more night to be with her. "We won't be able to meet with Vivian, the police and her attorney until the morning."

Her indecision was clear as she nibbled her lower lip, worrying it between her teeth.

When, at last, her gaze dipped to his mouth, he knew he'd won. Still, he wanted to hear her say it.

"Will you spend tonight with me, Nicole?" Not for anything could he have kept the growl out of his voice. "Let me touch you. Taste you. Make you feel good."

The rapid rise and fall of her breasts called to his hands. But still he waited for the words.

"I'd like that," she said finally, hovering closer until her long waves brushed his shoulder. Her dark eyes smoldered with new fire when she peered up at him again. "Yes. Please."

Ten

Her whole body hummed with anticipation as the car service deposited them in front of Desmond's modern stone-and-wood estate overlooking Lake Tahoe.

Nicole's gaze latched on his square shoulders as he unlocked the tall double doors at the entrance, the sight of him anchoring her. Somehow, knowing that she wasn't alone in this heady attraction, that he'd thought about their time together so much that he wanted another night with her, soothed the wound she'd felt to her feminine pride at the way things ended the first time. Dragging in a breath of cool mountain air, she noted the remote feel of the property before she followed him inside, the trees close on every side except for the back, where deep terraces provided patios for enjoying the waterfront. Desmond had pointed out the casino he owned on their way through town, less than a mile from his house.

Now, she stood to one side of the open-concept living and dining area, leaving room for the driver to bring things inside while Desmond flipped switches to turn on lights and close blinds. All around her, the banks of windows were soundlessly shuttered, folding them in privacy. Pendant lamps blinked on over a long island wrapped in gray quartz near the dining room, followed by a lamp in a downstairs suite she could see into thanks to the open door. A white brick fireplace taking up a whole wall in the bedroom brightened with the leap of gas flames before Desmond set aside the home remote.

He thanked the driver and sent the man on his way. Desmond closed the door behind him, then re-armed the alarm before toeing off his leather dress shoes on the front mat.

And somehow the sight of sock-clad feet on the hardwood floor as he neared Nicole made what they were about to do the most real to her. There was something intimate about that small, private act of removing his shoes. Making himself comfortable to be with her.

"Nicole." He strode toward her, shrugging off his jacket and flipping it onto one of two low barrel chairs in the living room. "Don't be nervous." He stopped just short of her, relieving her of the leather bag she still clutched by the shoulder strap. He set it on the chair near his jacket. "It's not too late to change your mind."

His hands slid around her upper arms, where too many layers—her blazer and the sleeves of her dress—prevented her from feeling the texture of his palms as he touched her.

"I'm not nervous anymore." Her heart thumped faster, everything inside her accelerating like she'd just put her foot on the gas. Her breath. The hot rush of blood in her veins. The leap of nerve endings.

"Were you before?" His focus lasered in on her as he lowered his hands from her. Instead, he flicked open the buttons on his shirtsleeves then folded back the cuffs. "Is everything okay?"

His thoughtfulness of her feelings shouldn't make her feel even more fluttery inside than his touch. But she couldn't deny she appreciated the way he checked in with her.

She told herself not to get attached to this. To the way he made her feel. But she had no way of knowing if she would take her own advice.

"I might have been a little nervous that nothing could top the way you made me feel last time," she admitted in a rush before she could stop herself. She laid her hand on his chest, feeling his heart thump steadily through the starched cotton of his white shirt. "I wondered if maybe I embellished it in my head because it was the first I'd been with someone in…a long while."

She'd come up with a million and one reasons to account for why she'd let herself go so completely with him. The months of overwhelming responsibilities, the grief of losing her sister, the fear of not providing everything Matthew needed. No doubt she'd been battling through a rough time in her life. And maybe that accounted for why being with Desmond had been so incredible. It had been a release valve for all that.

"I'm sorry that you worried for even a minute." His hands flexed gently around her arms. Up to her shoulders. His thumbs brushed her collarbone before they dipped inside her jacket, spreading the lapels wider to give him access to her neck. His lips fastened on a spot just below her ear, his tongue flicking lightly before he spoke against her damp flesh. "I promise you the first time wasn't a fluke."

Her knees wobbled a little, and she gripped the fabric of his shirt, steadying herself in the rush of pleasure warming her skin. Not just where he kissed, either. Liquid heat flooded her senses.

"I believe you." She shivered as he pushed her jacket down and off her shoulders.

"Good." He kissed a path along her jaw, ending at the corner of her lips. He nipped the lower one before he drew on it. When he broke the contact, he tucked a finger under her chin and tipped her face up to his. "Tonight's going to be so much better."

She felt the truth of the promise in the electric current running through her. She might not trust him with her heart or her feelings, but she absolutely trusted him with her pleasure. And after the way she'd shouldered so much on her own these last months, it was a heady gift to be able to hand that off to this sexy, capable man staring at her like she was the most appealing woman he'd ever laid eyes on.

"You set the bar high." Dragging her fingers lightly down his chest, she sketched the ridges of his abs. "I have a lot of good memories from last time."

He let go of her chin and plucked her hand from where she'd veered close to his belt. He took his time threading his fingers through hers, interlocking them.

"Multiply that by all the extra hours we have before the sun rises, and you'll see why it's easy to be confident you're going to be thoroughly…" He leaned close again to speak into her ear, the huff of his breath a teasing stroke. "Pleasured."

Oh.

The math of hours and pleasures was almost as enticing as the feel of his body close to hers as he led her toward the bedroom with the fireplace. She tried to focus on that and not the way he'd deliberately put her at ease, making sure she was comfortable. Because if she thought too much about him beyond the delicious release he could give her, she risked getting lost in feelings she wasn't ready for.

Feelings he refuses to share, a cruel voice in her head whispered.

But she refused to let that rob her of this night with him. She deserved it. Hell, after what she'd been through this year, she *needed* it.

In the bedroom, he let go of her hand to shut the door, and she gathered up her hair before presenting him her back.

"Unzip me?" she asked over her shoulder, little tremors of eagerness racing through her.

She liked the way his eyes blazed with an internal heat. And she definitely liked that he allowed his attention to travel the length of her body.

A moment later, he closed the distance between them. He wrapped one strong arm around her, drawing her against him so his hips notched against the back of hers. She gasped at the feel of him, his need for her deliciously evident as he tugged down the long zipper of her black knit dress.

He let the fabric fall away as it parted, his breath tickling against bare skin while he shoved the material down and over her hips until it fell at her feet. She let go of her hair to stroke his forearm where it was wrapped around her waist. She glimpsed them together in a whitewashed cheval mirror, their bodies lit by the orange flames from the fireplace, her hair tousled and unruly. But while she was halfway to naked save for her simple black undergarments and boots, Desmond remained fully clothed. White dress shirt folded back at the forearms, he still wore dark wool gabardine pants that teased the backs of her thighs.

"Keep looking," he breathed into her ear, his gray gaze meeting hers in the glass. His fingers trailed down her hip to trace the elastic of her panties. "And you'll see how much you like me touching you."

Powerless to look away, she watched. A riot of sensation rocked her as his touch descended lower, sliding under the waistband of her underwear. When his other arm banded around her, higher on her rib cage, he cupped her breasts through the sheer fabric of her bra, teasing the tips to tight, hard points.

Trapped against him in the best possible way, she panted with the sensual onslaught, her eyes sliding closed to lose herself to the skilled, seductive plucking of his fingers.

"No." His sharp command was a whisper in her ear, the word damp on her skin. "Keep watching." His voice had a jagged edge over his rough breathing, as if he was as affected by the touch as her. "It's the hottest, sexiest thing I've ever seen. I haven't been able to stop thinking about what you look like when you come apart for me."

Tension coiled tighter between her thighs. She hauled her eyes open again, mesmerized by the sight but too caught up in the slick pressure of his fingers right where she needed him most.

"Please." She didn't know if she wanted him to take her to the precipice faster or slower. Wasn't sure if she wanted the sweet thrill in her body to find an

outlet or to remain in this breathless, perfect anticipation forever. "It feels so—"

She broke off, the build of tension arching her
back. Robbing her ability to speak. Slamming her
eyes closed.

"That's it." He praised her with hoarse satisfaction as his fingers plunged inside her. "That's what
I've been dreaming about every night."

Her release shattered her, rocking her body and
turning her knees to liquid. She would have fallen
if not for being pinned to him, his hands never ceas-
ing their carnal work, calling forth every last spasm
from her shuddering form. When at last he slowed
to a stop, he turned her in his arms before carrying
her boneless form to the bed, pausing only to peel
off her boots. She wanted to protest, to give him the
same incredible fulfillment he'd just provided for
her, but her words died in her throat as she slivered
her eyes open to see him undressing.

He'd never been in such a hurry to be naked.

Desmond tore off his shirt with a muttered oath,
needing to be inside the tousled siren who twisted
in his bed covers, reaching toward him with hungry
hands. His control had started slipping about the time
she'd asked him to unzip her. By now the tattered
remnants of it had barely enough strength to remind
him to find a condom before giving up the ghost.

Later, he'd wonder how she wielded this kind of
power over him. At this moment, he could only scav-

enge the wherewithal to locate the necessary protection and sheathe himself while she shimmied out of the sheer black underthings that had made him forget his own name. Then again, seeing her naked was even more potent, her red hair trailing over her shoulders to frame the perfect curves of her breasts. He kneed one slender thigh wider, making room for himself where he most wanted to be.

Levering over her, he was poised to sink inside her when she cupped his jaw.

"This is the part I've been dreaming about," she whispered, echoing his words back to him. "You. Filling me."

His need unleashed. He sank inside her fully, driven by her words. Her thighs clamped around his waist like a vise, her hips lifted to him. For him. Over and over again, he took what she offered and gave her more. All of him.

She moaned and whimpered, urged him on with a train of hungry demands in his ear. He lost himself in her, straining closer to the pleasure that he'd only ever find with her.

The thought blindsided him. Slowed his thrusts for one protracted moment while his heart hammered in his chest, blood rushing in his ears. Her passion-fogged eyes met his, her bee-stung lips full and damp from his kisses and bites. Seeing her that way, knowing she was every bit as lost as him, was the tether that kept him in the moment. The realization that made him need to deliver on every sensual promise. To give her everything she wanted.

He lowered his mouth to her breast, drawing hard on the pebbled peak. Her hips bucked against him, arching closer. Angling. Sensing what she needed, he reached between them to touch the place certain to send her flying. He circled the tender flesh while he thrust faster, harder, pushing them both higher.

When her back arched this time, tension curving her spine, he was ready. The soft pulls of her feminine flesh squeezed him, and he let himself go with her. On and on her body worked his, one shudder calling forth another until they were both spent and damp. Sated and replete.

For now, at least.

Desmond knew that just lying beside her would incite his hunger again, all too soon. So for now, he wrapped her close to him, holding her without questioning the need that seemed to have written itself in his soul.

He breathed through the idea, telling himself it was over-the-top and nonsensical to think so. Knowing better all the while. He respected the way she championed her nephew, the way she protected him and put her whole life on hold to make sure she got the answers she needed about the boy.

But the torment of his thoughts eased as Nicole nestled sweetly against him, her silky hair a warm blanket on the side of his chest where she lay under one arm. He wasn't going to question the rise of unexpected feelings where she was concerned. Not when he could breathe in the apple scent of her shampoo and stroke the smooth curve of her hip.

He admired her strength. Was grateful for the way she loved and advocated for a boy that Desmond should have been protecting all this time. He'd always felt indebted to Zach for giving him the courage to stand up to his father, and yet he'd let him down by failing to look out for his heir. And yes, he felt sure in his gut that Matthew was Zach's kid. He would do whatever it took to help the boy from here on out. And Nicole, too, as his guardian.

She won't welcome your help.

He remembered how defensive she'd been about preserving her role in Matthew's life, warning him she wouldn't give up her guardianship "no matter the financial incentive." Not that he would contest it, of course. But if she was that prickly about accepting help, it would make his path forward uncomfortable.

He kissed Nicole's damp forehead and vowed to uphold the promise he'd made to give her this night of pleasure. That much, at least, he could provide.

And, he hoped, whatever they shared tonight would soften her for the moment when she realized Desmond would need a place in Matthew's life if the boy was truly Zach's son. As the long-lost heir of Desmond's best friend, Nicole's nephew would become his highest priority. That was an obligation Desmond would never relinquish.

Not even if it put him at odds with the woman in his arms.

Eleven

Nerves stretched taut the next morning, Nicole sat beside Desmond in the interview room at the correctional facility in Nevada City. They'd been subject to security screening after the hour-long drive from Desmond's house, but apparently the meeting place was more secure for the group than at the local lockup in Truckee.

She sipped the tea a kind corrections officer had brought for her while they waited at a conference table. The room was sparsely institutional, with cream-colored walls and a mirror that they'd been informed was a viewing panel, even though they'd been assured no one watched on the other side. The meeting would be recorded, however, since Vivian

Fraser had promised information about Alec the police would find helpful, according to her attorney.

Did she plan to throw her former lover under the
bus for the crimes she'd committed? Even Desmond
had questioned whether Vivian would have acted
alone to threaten Chiara and hack the influencer's
social media accounts. Or did Vivian plan to accuse
Alec of some other crime?

The tea was barely warm, but the orange pekoe
flavor provided a welcome distraction from the tension that had been growing between her and Desmond ever since breakfast. Their morning had
been awkwardly polite and cool after the night had
stripped her defenses bare. She'd followed the scent
of pancakes to the kitchen and been ready to wrap
her arms around his waist. Rub her cheek against
his broad back. Absorb his strength and warmth the
way she had all night long. Except then he'd turned
around and greeted her with a formal good morning
that left her reeling.

Her appetite had vanished, and the nervous
knot in her stomach had started twisting and never
stopped. Luckily, she'd been able to spend their car
ride texting with a counselor from Matthew's school
and making arrangements for a parent conference
next week. Nothing urgent, the administrator had
insisted. Just to check in after the tumultuous personal year Matthew had experienced. The exchange
had helped her put the day in perspective, reminding her of her priorities. Nothing was more impor-

tant than making sure Matthew was well adjusted and had whatever help he needed to cope with the changes in his life. As much as she wanted to find her nephew's father, that task came second to his emotional health.

She wouldn't let the hole in her chest with Desmond's name on it keep her from returning to San Jose and the life she had there. Desmond had backed off after their time together. Again. And that spoke volumes about how he viewed her. She'd gone into the evening thinking she was going to focus on the physical. But even though he'd delivered every ounce of pleasure she could have ever imagined, Nicole had discovered a wellspring of tender new emotions underneath the physical connection.

After the way he'd flipped the switch on that this morning—retreating once more—she now understood that she wouldn't be able to share that kind of encounter ever again. Physical pleasure didn't exist without deeper emotion behind it. At least, not for her. She'd only been fooling herself to think otherwise.

The door to the interview room swung wide a moment later by a trim, uniformed female officer leading the way for a petite brunette in a prison jumpsuit two sizes too large for her. Behind her, a burly older man in an olive-green suit strode in carrying a briefcase. A second officer brought up the rear, a middle-aged guy with thinning blond hair that had been carefully combed.

While the officer shared names and explained the interview was being recorded, Nicole studied Vivian in the seat across from her. In the stories about Alec's assistant online, she'd been a redhead, but now there was no hint of the color or her former curls. But even with no makeup and the orange jumpsuit, Vivian remained a lovely woman. She possessed delicate features and graceful movements, although her eyes were shrewdly assessing when they landed on Nicole.

The officer leading the meeting, Lieutenant Bragg, opened the floor to Vivian, who glanced briefly at her attorney before beginning to speak. Unfortunately, Nicole missed her opening words because Desmond's hand crept over to hers underneath the table. The warmth of his palm covered the back of hers where it rested in her lap, and she felt another piece of her heart slide into his keeping, even though he'd made it clear he didn't want any such thing.

"The long and short of it," Vivian was saying when Nicole was able to dial back into her words, "is that Alec promised to bail me out if I'd take the fall for him for hacking Chiara Campagna's social media. I knew it might take him a couple of days to make that happen, but now that it's been weeks, I know he has no intention of following through on that promise."

The male officer interrupted her, leaning forward so that his tie clip clunked against the conference table. "Are you suggesting Alec Jacobsen hacked into Ms. Campagna's accounts and threatened her?"

The lawyer began to bluster about immunity and protecting Vivian's rights, but the prisoner resumed speaking. It worked to quiet the others since she had the microphone.

"I have kept Alec's secrets for fourteen years because I—" She stopped herself. Made a wry, angry face that twisted her features. "That is, I *used to* love him. But I won't protect him any longer, and I'm done keeping his secrets. Alec stole Zach's art and ideas for his video game. He knew about Zach's child and needed to prevent Zach's heir from claiming intellectual property theft."

Nicole didn't realize she'd gasped until all eyes swiveled toward her. Desmond shifted his chair closer to hers in order to drape a protective arm around her shoulders. The weight and the warmth of him helped her steady her breathing. She clasped a hand around the gold pendant she wore that had belonged to her sister, the one containing Matthew's photo as a baby.

Zach Eldridge was Matthew's father.

"How do you know for certain?" Nicole managed finally, questioning the woman directly. "About Zach's child?"

At this, Vivian turned to her attorney, but the older man nodded.

The prisoner's eyes met hers. "Alec hacked Zach's email and read all the exchanges between Zach and Lana. The notes made it clear they were having an affair and that Lana broke up with Zach when she found out she was pregnant." She shrugged as she shifted in her seat. "Maybe she grew a conscience? Or maybe she realized it would be uncool to raise a kid with a student. I don't remember her exact reasoning."

"You saw the emails?" Nicole asked, wondering if this woman's testimony would be enough to prove that Zach was Matthew's father. Then again, maybe she would say anything, considering she was under arrest and seeking a deal.

"I read some of them," Vivian admitted, her dark hair falling forward as she leaned over the microphone on the table. "Alec liked showing them to me to prove he was recovered from his crush on Lana. Alec and Zach were both fascinated with her, and all three of them hung out a lot the summer before she started working at the school." The woman's eyes flicked to Desmond as she explained, "At first, Zach and Lana were just friends, because Zach thought he was gay. But then she started seeing Zach alone, and things heated up between them before school started. It sounded like Lana tried to put an end to it once she began student teaching at Dowdon."

At least she'd had some scruples about that, Nicole thought with a sliver of relief. It had upset her to think Lana would have approached a student in her care, no matter how close their ages, but if the friendship had begun earlier, it was at least a little more understandable. Nicole wondered how her sister had met the boys that summer, but it had been a small town. They could have crossed paths most anywhere.

Before she could ask any questions, Vivian continued.

"Anyway, Alec turned sort of bitter about it because he was honoring Lana's wishes to stay away and Zach still met up with her. Alec started keeping tabs on them so obsessively, I figured he still liked her. Plus Alec started keeping notes on Zach's idea for a video game, always prodding Zach to think through all the different levels of the game and what should happen for the battles." Her expression grew more animated, eyes widening. "Zach's ideas were brilliant."

Nicole felt Desmond tense beside her. His grip tightened on hers.

"Are you saying the whole game was Zach's idea?" Desmond asked in a tone that might sound composed to someone who didn't know him. But Nicole heard the anger underneath.

She felt a cold, indignant rage of her own growing. A sickness, even, at the idea of how people could quietly hurt those they professed to care about.

"Pretty much." Vivian shrugged. "Although before you get any worse ideas about Alec, he was as devastated as anyone when Zach died. Their friendship might have been in a weird place, but Alec admired his genius. He immortalized it with the game."

There was something so wrong in that statement, so out-of-touch with human emotions and what real friendship meant, that Nicole felt ill. How could Zach's so-called friend have kept his "brilliant" mind a secret all those years, soaking up the adulation of fans and game critics for work that hadn't been his own? Worse, how could he have purposely cheated an innocent child out of learning about his father?

The room wobbled a little. She *really* didn't feel well.

"Will you excuse me?" she murmured, relinquishing Desmond's hand in a sudden need for air as the room closed in on her. Her vision narrowed to pinpricks of images in front of her while her heart raced. "I'm so sorry." Standing, she lurched for the door while chairs scraped back around the table to follow her. Or maybe help her. "Please. Finish without me. I just need—"

Her remaining vision blurred a bit as she pushed through the door and into the hall.

A strong arm gripped her. Steadying her.

"I've got you."

She didn't need to look to know Desmond was beside her. His voice anchored her. His scent, so achingly familiar by now, felt more comforting than it should. Especially since, now that she had the answers she needed about Matthew, she would have no reason to see Desmond again.

That wasn't the reason for her panic. But it didn't help.

"I'll just splash some cold water on my face, and be out before you know it." She needed a time-out.

From Vivian. From the hurt she felt for her sister, her nephew.

For herself.

Her stomach knotted tighter. Glancing up, she saw the door to the ladies' room nearby and threw herself toward it. Out of his grasp. "I'm fine. I'll be fine." Maybe if she said it enough times, she could make it true. "I just need a minute."

"Are you sure you're okay?" Desmond asked Nicole on the car ride to his home two hours later.

He regretted not hiring a car service for the trip so he could have given her his undivided attention, but that morning he'd been so amped up after their night together that he thought driving his own Range Rover would give him a way to stay busy. Now, when he kept turning anxious eyes to Nicole to scan her pale face, he hated that she wasn't his sole focus.

He hadn't trusted her not to faint and hit her head in the bathroom by herself, and he'd had every intention of remaining by her side. But a woman who worked at the security checkpoint at the correctional facility had intervened, insisting she would make sure Nicole was safe.

He'd waited outside the bathroom for fifteen minutes, until Nicole had opened the door long enough to ask him to please finish the interview without her. She couldn't look at Vivian Fraser again after the things the woman had admitted.

Thankfully, Vivian hadn't protested the absence,

since the woman had conveyed the main point she'd wanted Nicole to hear. Matthew was Zach's son. She'd promised digital access to some of the emails that would prove it, as she'd kept an old hard drive in a safe-deposit box to protect herself in case Alec didn't bail her out as he'd promised. Desmond had related everything he could remember to Nicole for the first half of their trip home, but she'd gone silent afterward.

"I'm fine." She'd said that more than once back at the jail, but he had yet to believe it. Her head tipped against the passenger side window, her eyes sliding closed. "Just tired after the emotional upheaval. I don't know if I really had a panic attack like Heidi—the woman who sat with me in the women's room—believed, but it was scary. I suddenly felt like I couldn't breathe even though all I was doing was breathing."

Guilt for what she'd been through—not just today, but for all the weeks she'd worked to uncover the truth about her nephew's father—was a ten-ton weight on his shoulders. He hadn't seen the truth that had been right in front of him for years because of misplaced loyalty that Alec Jacobsen had never deserved.

Hearing how Alec had worked to undermine Zach, and later Matthew, had detonated inside him, decimating his old beliefs and trust. The damage to the Mesa Falls partnership—which would require legal intervention to buy out Alec's share—was the least of Desmond's concerns. He hated that Zach's heir had gone thirteen years without knowing the people who'd loved Zach.

"I'm so damned sorry I didn't recognize that Alec was a lying, dangerous bastard. Even sorrier that I stood in your way while you were trying to find out the truth for yourself." Grip tightening on the steering wheel, he took the access road that led to his home. "Vivian admitted she was the one who got you fired when you were working at the ranch after the holidays, by the way. Alec knew you were asking questions and interceded."

Another fact their private investigator hadn't turned up. But then, Alec had seen to it that the supervisor who'd fired Nicole was let go—and paid well to take an extended overseas vacation—the next day. One more failure that was on Desmond's shoulders.

"I'm just glad to go home," Nicole admitted, her attention still focused out the window. "My questions served their purpose to get things moving. Alec started making mistakes, which is how we finally learned the truth." She turned to him as the Range Rover climbed the incline toward his property. "Don't you think it's strange that Alonzo Salazar knew about Matthew and never told you?"

"I'm guessing Lana never revealed the father's name. If she never told you, why would she tell the teacher who oversaw her? Alonzo probably just wanted to help her with the child since he knew she was raising Matthew alone." Desmond remembered so many ways his old mentor had guided him through the worst year of his life, helping a devastated kid find his way. "He was good like that."

"It was a kindness I can never repay, since Matthew has thrived at his school." She twisted the gold pendant that hung from the chain around her neck. "With any luck, I can borrow against a future settlement of Matthew's claim the game *Hooves of Thunder* was stolen from his father. Even if he only wins a small share of the proceeds, it will certainly cover his tuition."

Desmond had never been so grateful to reach his house before, because he needed to put the vehicle in Park to turn and address what she'd just said. Something that had raked over his every last nerve.

"Nicole." He switched off the ignition for good measure, buying himself a few extra moments to make sure he approached this conversation the right way. "You don't need to borrow a cent. As Zach's heir, Matthew now owns a share of Mesa Falls, effective as soon as I contact a lawyer to draw up the paperwork. The ranch has operated at a profit for years."

She tensed in the passenger seat, her hands sliding into her lap, fingers twisting together.

"Zach was never an owner of the ranch. We're not interested in charity, just what Matthew is legally entitled to." Her words, softly spoken, cut straight through him.

On a day of hurt and anger, that her refusal of his help sliced him deeper than anything else was a testament to how much she'd come to mean to him. He had to swallow past the ball of pain in his chest.

"Everything we worked for in Montana was because of Zach. Because we couldn't save him. Because we loved him, respected him and hated that the last days he spent with us—time that we were *supposed* to be helping him forget about his problems—ended with his death." The wound had never healed. Desmond had just built his life around the hole in him, but it would always be there. "He saved me, Nicole. Caring for his son is not charity. It's a debt."

Something like understanding, or maybe just a temporary need to appease him, lit her dark eyes. She returned to twisting her fingers, locking them together at one angle and then another.

"I understand why you feel that way," she said quietly, her whole slim body still. "But you've already offered to retain a lawyer to help Matthew with his claim. That's more than enough. I didn't travel to Montana so you'd rewrite your whole business. I just wanted to know the truth about Matthew's father. And now that I do, we can go back to our lives."

The hits kept coming. He shouldn't be surprised.

He'd retreated from her just this morning because he didn't want to give her the wrong impression, but now he wondered if that hadn't been an act of self-preservation as much as anything. He'd known all along she might not accept his help where her nephew was concerned.

"You're in that much of a hurry to leave?" He studied her face, regretting that they had to have this conversation now when she'd admitted she was tired. When they'd both had hellish days.

"I think it would be wisest. Last night made it difficult for me to remember what we are to each other on a day-to-day basis." A flash of hurt might have streaked over her expression, but it was gone again before he could be sure. "There's no sense pretending that spending time together will lead anywhere."

Damn it, he hadn't meant to hurt her.

Just thinking that he might have only added to the weight of guilt threatening to drown him. He would do anything to fix that. He owed her everything for stepping in to care for Matthew.

A boy he hadn't even met.

The wrongs he'd done kept adding up as it occurred to him that he needed to meet Zach's son. But first, he had to keep Nicole here long enough to figure out the best way to make that happen.

"Spending time together could help us iron out the problems we're discussing right now." He started to reach for her. "Matthew's guardianship—"

"Is not up for debate," she said sharply, pulling back. "I've been clear about that from the beginning."

Hell.

He wished he could bring her inside so they could

talk over dinner, but he feared as soon as she left the vehicle, she'd start packing. It was his fault for putting this wall between them again. He shouldn't have been so adamant about managing expectations in their relationship, but he'd been afraid of hurting her.

Unfortunately, he'd done just that anyway.

"I understand." He reached for her hands again, covering them with his. When she didn't pull away, he stroked the back of one, reminding himself he wasn't going to have another chance with her. He needed to find a way to maintain a dialogue with her and protect Zach's son at the same time. He owed it to Zach. To Nicole, for turning her whole life upside down to step into her sister's shoes and be a mother to Matthew. "I'd never question your right as a parent."

A fraction of the tension seemed to ease from her.

Her hands stilled.

"Thank you." She let out a long breath. "It's a lot of responsibility. I'm just trying to do my best with him. He's such a great kid. He deserves to be happy and secure. Loved."

Hearing her speak helped Desmond see that he wanted the same thing. Matthew's happiness and security had become the most important thing in his world today. And considering that the responsibility weighed heavily on Nicole—no matter how much she loved the boy—made Desmond realize he wanted to offer a more concrete kind of help.

There had to be a way he could ensure the boy's future…

The answer hit him hard. Legally, there was a way to make sure Matthew had every financial advantage and future protection. A way to ease the burden on Nicole so she could spend her time being a guardian instead of worrying about paying tuition or facilitating her nephew's legal recognition as Zach's heir. But would Nicole ever consent to it? Desmond recalled with unease how she'd refused to accept his offers of financial help. He didn't want to be at odds with her, but he was out of time to figure out how to best appeal to her.

"I agree with you." The more he thought about his idea, the more he liked it. The more it seemed like the simplest solution. "Matthew should be happy and secure. And he has the right to know more about his father while maintaining the same attachment to you that he's always had."

One auburn eyebrow lifted. Curious.

His heart pounded in anticipation of sharing his plan. He hoped she would at least hear him out because his intentions were good. Desmond had never considered taking on such a big role in a child's life before, but this was Zach Eldridge's kid they were talking about. A boy who'd been overlooked for far too long by the people who loved Zach.

"What do you mean?"

He dug deep to offer her words he'd never thought he'd say to anyone.

"Marry me, Nicole."

Twelve

"Excuse me?"

Shifting on the leather bucket seat in the front of Desmond's Range Rover, Nicole needed that last thing he'd said repeated. She had zoned out during the panic attack back at the jail, so she guessed she could be having a recurrence of whatever had happened then.

Because Desmond couldn't have possibly proposed.

"You'd maintain complete say over raising Matthew, of course," he continued, speaking in a rush, as if he had a lot to say. "But legally, a marriage would give Matthew immediate financial security along with my name. We could spend part of the year at the ranch so he could get to know—"

"Are you suggesting a marriage between…*us*?" She didn't want to presume when she still felt disconnected and confused. Her whole life had changed—again—after today's visit to the jail, and she hadn't come close to wrapping her head around what it meant.

"Yes. Between you and me." He seemed to slow himself down with an effort. "I think it would be beneficial for all of us. Matthew especially."

Her heart fell. There'd been no misunderstanding after all. No feelings. No connection.

Realizing his hand still rested on hers, she tugged her fingers free. She couldn't afford to indulge in the feel of his touch—something that had offered such comfort a moment ago—when he was making a mockery of their whole relationship by suggesting this bloodless arrangement that would apparently benefit Matthew.

She wanted to yell. To screech, *How dare you?* right into his oh-so-composed, far-too-handsome face illuminated by the dash lights. But doing that would let him see how much this coldhearted contract hurt.

"I thought you had no aspirations to fatherhood." She remembered his exact phrasing, because it had punctured a hole in the stupid balloon of hopes that she'd somehow allowed to expand too far, too fast. "I don't think Matthew deserves a figurehead father who isn't really interested in filling the role."

She saw the remark make a direct hit, but it gave

her zero satisfaction considering Desmond looked genuinely distraught at the thought. On some level at least, he cared enough to not want to inflict hurt.

"You're right," he told her quickly, recovering. The muscle in his jaw flexed. "He deserves better than that. Better than me. But I'm here. I'm just trying to figure out how to cover a lot of concerns, and I'm not doing that effectively by strategizing in a hurry."

The hollow in her chest echoed with the empty proposal, already withdrawn. Or as good as. Clearly, he understood why it wasn't a workable idea. But it still hurt that he would have suggested something guaranteed to break her heart by reminding her of all that Desmond wasn't interested in pursuing with her.

Love. Happiness. Family.

They may not have known each other long, but she already understood him well enough to know she couldn't settle for a fraction of the affection he was capable of giving. No matter how incendiary their lovemaking had been. He had far more to give than what he'd offered to her. And she wouldn't sign on to a relationship that made it easy for someone she cared about to walk away from her again. Her mother's defection had shown her how much that could level her.

"There's no need to rush only to have regrets later," she assured him, needing to end this conversation and put distance between them before he saw how much his suggestion had rattled her. How much it tweaked the foolish feelings she'd developed for him. "We can communicate long-distance and arrange a time for you to meet Matthew. Maybe one day, when he's a little older, he can visit Montana and meet all of his father's friends."

She wanted that for Mattie. He deserved to see for himself how much his father had been loved and respected by the Mesa Falls owners, Alec notwithstanding.

"One day? Nicole, I'm serious about wanting to meet him sooner than that." His gray eyes were sincere. Hurt, even? "I'd like to spend some time getting to know him."

Her fingers gripped the leather upholstery to keep from reaching across the car for him. She couldn't bear to look into those gray depths and see feelings that he hadn't shared with her before. Feelings that—she reminded herself—were about her nephew. Not her.

Still, she wouldn't hold her misplaced love for Desmond against him. And yes, she knew it was love because it hurt so much to think about walking away from him. But she needed to do just that, sooner rather than later, to save herself an even deeper heartache sure to come from letting herself see an answering feeling in him that wasn't there.

"Of course you can see him." She conceded the point, wanting Matthew to know Desmond even if she couldn't be a part of his life anymore. "I will make sure that happens. Maybe at his school, where he's most comfortable."

Matthew was even more comfortable at home, with her, but no matter how much she loved her sister's son, she wouldn't be able to bear memories of Desmond in her house with them. Just imagining it for a moment threatened to make her throw her arms around his neck and ask him to reconsider his refusal to be a father.

His refusal to let her close to him.

Desmond started to speak, perhaps just to thank her, but the tears burning the backs of her eyelids were too hot. Too imminent.

For the second time that day, she had to excuse herself.

"I'm sorry, Desmond. I can't finish this right now." Levering open the passenger door of his SUV, she blinked away the worst of the coming flood. "I need to pack my things. It would be best if I return home now."

Thirteen

"It's strange being back here," Weston Rivera observed from the top bunk of a double dorm room at Dowdon School shortly before the anniversary gala fundraiser was due to begin.

Seated next to a window overlooking the grounds of their former boarding school, Desmond sipped his bourbon and tried not to ruin everyone else's evening with his sour mood. It was strange enough for him being *anywhere* without Nicole, but she'd returned to San Jose a week and a half ago, and he hadn't been able to stop thinking about her since. He missed her so much more than he would have ever expected.

Desmond glanced from Weston's tuxedo-clad legs hanging over the edge of the bunk to where Miles finished the knot in his bow tie at a mirror mounted over a study desk. Then his gaze continued to Gage doing pull-ups on the door frame between the en suite bath and the rest of the room, the New Zealander's breath whooshing out each time his chin reached the top of the door. He hadn't even put a shirt on yet.

Jonah Norlander was dressed and ready for the gala, the new father finishing up a video call with his wife and baby daughter on the far side of the room, rounding out the five friends who had flown in to support their alma mater and show the press their unity in condemning Alec Jacobsen. The story had leaked about the stolen game, and Alec's fall from grace had been swift and well publicized. Fortunately, the public seemed to feel almost as deceived and outraged as the Mesa Falls partners, so the backlash had landed squarely on Alec's shoulders. Business remained good at Mesa Falls and the partners were researching the best way to buy out Alec's share.

Questions about Zach had followed, with reporters racing to uncover the most facts first. Public opinion about Alonzo Salazar had shifted to the favorable when it was revealed his tell-all book had been an attempt to provide financial support for Zach's fatherless child. The gaming community was leading the way in championing Alonzo since interest in Zach's brief life—and his heir—was rabid now that his original drawings has been released. Nicole had issued a statement requesting privacy for her family, and it seemed to have been respected. Desmond had phoned Matthew's school to inquire if they wanted private security to help keep the boy and his classmates safe, but they'd assured him that they had all the necessary measures in place.

Making Desmond unnecessary there, too. Just like he'd been with Nicole. The empty space inside him yawned wider. Had it only been ten days since he'd seen her? It felt like ten years, every day dragging on forever. He'd been useless at the casino the week before, unable to think about anything but her.

"Damn right it's strange being back here," Gage announced as he finished the pull-ups and jumped to the floor. "The whole place shrank since we were kids." He toed the bottom bunk where he used to sleep. "I don't think I'd even fit in that thing now."

"If you ask me," Miles added, finishing his bow tie and turning away from the mirror, "it's good to be here tonight with people I know are my real friends. No more knives in our backs."

Weston leaped to the floor with a thud and scooped up the champagne bottle out of the ice bucket that someone from the school had delivered earlier as a thank-you for their donation. "I was going to say I'd drink to that, but I think it calls for something more potent. Gage, where are you hiding that bourbon?"

Desmond lifted the bottle from the arm of his chair and told himself to get with the program for his friends' sake. He might not have a knife in his back anymore thanks to Alec's arrest on the charge of harassing and hacking Chiara Campagna, but the hole in Desmond's chest still gaped thanks to Nicole. A sure sign she'd affected him far more deeply than he'd allowed himself to believe at first.

"Right here." Desmond passed the bottle to Wes. "I've already helped myself."

Jonah ambled over to join them as glasses were procured from the catering cart that had delivered the champagne. While his friends laughed, poured and passed the bottle, Desmond tried to dial in on the evening, even though he didn't feel much like celebrating when he hadn't heard a word from Nicole in ten days. He'd tried to give her space after he'd screwed up with that ill-advised marriage proposal. Even in his cluelessness, he'd read the misstep in her lovely features right away.

He'd hurt her, and that killed him.

And it hit him in a flash why he missed her so much, why he was at such loose ends. He understood why that pained him so much, because it turned out he'd fallen for her in spite of all his best precautions to make sure that didn't happen. The feeling made him want to surge to his feet and find her, fundraiser be damned.

He started to rise from the chair, then hesitated. Looking back on that final conversation with her, he couldn't help but wonder why it had hurt *her*, too? Was there even the smallest chance she'd developed feelings like the ones that had taken his legs out from under him?

Even if by some incredible coincidence she had, that didn't alleviate his biggest concern. *I don't think Matthew deserves a figurehead father who isn't really interested in the role.* Nicole had never been so right about anything. How could he be a father to Matthew—even if Nicole cared enough for Desmond to reconsider—when he didn't have the slightest idea how to be a father? He'd had the worst role model on the planet.

His heart grew heavier than ever. Love was supposed to make things better, wasn't it? Apparently not.

"Desmond, you're missing the toast, man." Miles's distinctive voice rasped the words as he leveled a glance at him. The others all had their glasses poured and lifted for a toast. "Get your glass over here now, then put yourself out of your misery and call Nicole afterward."

Straightening his jacket, Desmond joined the circle in the middle of the floor where they used to have epic Friday night wrestling matches.

"Clairvoyant now?" Desmond asked as he raised his drink.

Miles shook his head and—fortunately for him—didn't crack a smile. "More like I had that same expression on my face when Chiara left my ass to go back to Los Angeles a few weeks ago, and it wasn't a good look then, either."

Desmond recalled all too well. And somehow the guy had won her back, but Miles didn't understand everything that kept Desmond from being the right man for Nicole. With an effort, he shoved that aside long enough to focus on his friends.

"You're right." Desmond looked around the circle, meeting the eyes of each man there. "Tonight is about remembering Zach and how many good times we had. He left a hell of a legacy for a guy whose time was too short, and it's on us to celebrate what he gave us."

No one spoke, and he knew every person there was remembering how Zach had touched their lives. For Desmond, it had meant getting free of his abusive father. And his mom getting free, too.

"To Zach," Miles echoed a moment later, lifting his glass.

"And Salazar," Wes added, raising his. "No way we would have weathered the aftermath to stand here and drink to Zach tonight without him."

"Best father I ever had," Gage quipped, since his elitist old man had always made it clear how much Gage disappointed him. "I'll drink to that."

Jonah stepped in last with his glass, simply saying, "Always."

Shorthand for a whole hell of a lot since they'd made that toast around a long-ago campfire.

Desmond drank deep, finishing his bourbon, musing over the toasts while Gage cranked up a Bluetooth speaker to blast "The Boys Are Back in Town" while they filed out of the dorm room to join the anniversary gala in the main reception hall. Something about Gage's words—*Best father I ever had*—circled around Desmond's brain.

Alonzo had been like a dad in a lot of ways, making sure all of them got through the shock and grief of losing their friend. Because of Alonzo Salazar, Desmond was a successful man today. And, thanks to that success, he'd been able to contribute a lot to the shelters he'd worked with. Didn't that mean Desmond actually had a damned good role model for fatherhood after all?

The possibility cracked open a whole new world for him.

He just hoped Nicole would agree.

Because as soon as the formal part of the Dowdon School event finished—once Desmond put in his appearance to support Mesa Falls and his friends—he was getting in a car and driving north to San Jose. He wasn't going to let another day go by without seeing the woman he loved and missed and needed more than air.

Pencil scratching softly over her sketch pad, Nicole sat cross-legged on her bed to flesh out some ideas for a local agricultural client who needed graphics for their farm's website. Her bedside clock said it was 11:00 p.m., long after her evening call with Matthew from his boarding school, but sometimes she worked best at this hour.

Or maybe she'd just decided to work since it was the night of the Dowdon School anniversary gala and she needed to prevent herself from watching the Twitter feed showing photos of the guests.

She pressed harder, determined at least not to refresh the page on her laptop the way she might have already done a few times like a pathetic, heartbroken fool. Why did Desmond have to look so handsome in a tuxedo? The man looked like he'd been born wearing Hugo Boss, the custom fit tailored exactly to his mouthwatering physique. A body she'd never get to see again.

One she'd never hold again, or take comfort from—

The doorbell chimed, halting her pencil along with thoughts that weren't helping her emotional recovery from the man she couldn't have. Who would be ringing the bell at this hour? She'd thought the reporters had all dispersed days ago.

Sliding from the bed, she slipped a long, comfy cardigan over her soft camisole and pajama pants, comfort wear for her broken heart. She padded toward the door in the dark, not wanting whoever was outside to see her looking through the peephole…

Desmond.

She clapped a hand over her mouth, but maybe she'd already emitted a sound, because his deep voice resonated through the door.

"Nicole?" A muffled sound against the door. Like maybe he'd touched it or leaned against it. "I'm sorry it's late. I saw your lights were on, and I really need to talk to you."

Her heart started a frantic rhythm, as if it could leap through the door to get to the man on the other side. But her heart was not in charge tonight, damn it. She squeezed her eyes closed and told herself it would be wrong not to answer the door because she was afraid of…everything. Of somehow revealing what she felt for him. Of losing her self-respect if she flung herself against him.

He was still wearing the tuxedo from the gala. Glancing down at her camisole—the same one she'd been wearing when she'd picked up that video call the first time she'd seen him—she yanked the sides of her sweater closer together before releasing her hair from a lopsided ponytail. Then, cursing herself for caring, she was tempted to put it back up again, but she ended up tugging open the door instead.

He went still on her front step, his gray eyes fixing on her face.

She wasn't sure how long they stood there, locked in silent perusal. But belatedly remembering her manners, she scuttled back a step to make room for him to enter.

"Did you want to come in?" She found the hair tie in her sweater pocket and played with it, stretching it between her fingers. "It's cool out there."

"You're right. Thank you." Appearing to give himself a shake, he stepped over the threshold of her house, effectively ruining her living room for her forever since she'd never be able to see the spot without him in it.

He seemed larger than life here, his shoulders and height more suited to a Montana ranch than her simple bungalow. She didn't invite him any deeper into the house at first, but then, realizing she was being churlish, she waved him toward the kitchen. He silently followed.

"Can I get you anything to drink?" She switched the burner on under the teakettle, then realized she still carried her sketch pad.

She slid it onto the round table just big enough for two.

"No. Thank you. Don't go to any trouble on my account when I've interrupted your evening." He glanced down at the spiral-bound paper. "Is this your work?"

Pulling a mug from the cupboard to give her something to do, she felt her throat go dry at the sight of his strong hands smoothing over the border of the paper. A visceral memory of his palms stroking her nearly made her shiver.

Having him here in her kitchen was too much. The space was too small, and he was such a presence. She could smell a hint of his aftershave if she got close enough.

"It is." She shifted her attention to the drawings she'd made of wildflower varieties. "I'm doing design work for a local flower farm. I've been enjoying the job since plants were one of the first things

I ever drew, back when my father was gardening at your school."

She had happy memories there, growing closer to her dad in the months after her mother had left. She'd had a good conversation with her dad a few days ago, the first she could remember him talking about Lana for any length of time since her death. Her father had wanted to know everything Nicole had learned about Matthew's dad, and she considered that a good sign for his grieving.

"They're so lifelike," Desmond said as he studied the images. "You're obviously very talented."

"Thank you." She scooped a blend of chamomile and lavender tea into a strainer basket inside her mug, thinking there was a lot they didn't know about each other. He'd never seen her work. She'd never set foot in his casino resort, where he spent his primary professional time. But there was no reason for them to learn more about one another when they weren't part of each other's lives. "Please. Have a seat. Tell me why you're here."

His hand fisted and he tapped the counter lightly with his knuckles before he moved to the café-style table and took a seat while Nicole poured her tea.

"I've missed you, Nicole."

The words surprised her so much she nearly sloshed the hot water over the side of the cup as she settled it on the table. Biting the inside of her cheek against the emotions he stirred inside her, she met his eyes across the table.

"That surprises me when you were very clear about the boundaries of our relationship. Or do you mean you miss the physical aspect? Which isn't really the same as missing *me*." She hadn't realized how much hurt she'd harbored about that—about his ability to pull away from her the morning after their incredible night together at his house.

"I miss *you*." His focus zeroed in on her, as if he'd thought about it a great deal. "It was stupid of me to try and dictate how our relationship should move forward instead of just enjoying the privilege of getting to know you. Getting close to you."

The warmth in his gaze was too much, and she wasn't ready for it when she didn't understand what he wanted or why he was really here. She took her time lifting the herbs from the tea and settling the metal strainer in a finger bowl she kept on the table for that purpose.

When she finished, she could only lift the cup to her lips and wait for him to continue. Her throat was dry at the possibility that he'd missed her. She'd missed him so much. Not just his touch, either, but his voice, his thoughts, his concern for her that had felt genuine in spite of everything. He'd tried to sit with her in a jailhouse ladies' room when she hadn't felt well. If that wasn't thoughtful, she didn't know the meaning of the word.

"But that wasn't the worst thing I did." He dragged his chair closer to hers. Right next to hers. "I can't tell you how many times I've regretted my unwise proposal. Not that I didn't want to be in your world every day and take care of you and Matthew forever, because I did. What I regret is that I let you think for a minute I only asked you so that I could provide legal benefits that I would have found a way to provide anyhow."

Blinking through the maze of words, she set her mug down, the scents of lavender and chamomile not strong enough to mask the sandalwood aftershave that strengthened in the steam from her cup.

"I'm sure I did not misunderstand you when you asked," she said carefully, wondering if he could have really meant the part about wanting to be in her world every day. That had sounded decidedly good.

More romantic than practical. More caring than dutiful.

"You didn't misunderstand." He reached to shift the mug farther away, then took both her hands in his, his warmth enveloping her. "I was the one who didn't comprehend anything. I was the one telling myself that I could keep you with me if I trotted out some lame arrangement that would provide you a material benefit instead of just admitting—to myself and to you—that I love you."

Fourteen

Nicole searched Desmond's face, knowing now she must have dreamed it all.

Of course she was dreaming. She must have fallen asleep drawing and somehow conjured the most hopeful longings of her heart to have the man she craved show up in her kitchen—wearing a tuxedo, no less—and saying words she secretly yearned to hear.

Desmond Pierce was a business tycoon who circulated in a totally different world from the one she inhabited, where her sole financial splurge was good tea. Glancing down at his hand clasping hers, a part of the dream she wanted to be real almost as much as the words he'd just spoken to her, Nicole swallowed hard and forced herself to blink. To wake up from imaginings that were all the more cruel for how impossible they were in reality.

"Nicole?" That sexy, deep voice of his tripped over her skin like a caress. His free hand slid under her hair to wrap around the back of her neck, cradle her head. "Say something, sweetheart. Did you hear what I said? Do you think there is any chance, in time, you might return those feelings?"

The sensation of his fingers in her hair couldn't possibly have been fabricated by her tired imaginings. The effect on her body was sweetly wicked, stirring things only this man had ever made her feel.

"Please tell me I'm not dreaming." She took his hand, the one that still held hers, and brought it to her cheek, needing reassurance that her heart hadn't tricked her. "Did you really just say—"

"I. Love. You." Gray eyes bored into hers with an intensity she couldn't mistake. A heat and tenderness that were so much better than any pale fantasy. "Just give me a chance to be in your life and I'll show you how much."

Her heart surged with happiness, emotions thick in her throat. If only she could be trust what she was feeling. She needed to understand.

"I have feelings for you." She'd known that she loved him that last night they'd spent together. That's why the cool morning after had hurt so much. "But you said you couldn't—that you'd never be a father."

Cold reality sliced back into her chest.

"I couldn't have been more wrong about that." He

lowered his hands to stroke over her shoulders. Her arms. "I thought I had the worst possible father—I did, actually. But I thought I'd never have anything to offer a child after what I went through, and I didn't want to taint someone with that."

He hadn't told her much about his youth, but the torture in his voice communicated a world of pain. She was grateful for the glimpse inside him, even if he shut it down quickly.

"I'm sorry. Every child deserves to be safe and loved." She slid her hand beneath his jacket to stroke his chest through the tuxedo shirt. "But you have so much more to offer a family than the legacy of the monster who raised you."

"I know that now." He covered her hand with his, then lifted it to his lips to kiss the back. Then he flipped it to kiss the palm. "While I was at the gala tonight with my partners, feeling like my world had ended because you were gone, someone raised a toast to Alonzo. And we got talking about what he did for us. How much he taught us. It was like someone flipped a switch and lit up a neon sign to remind me I could look outside my gene pool for inspiration. That I had a damned good father figure and that I could be one, too."

The last of her reservations dissolved at the certainty in his voice, relief and joy for herself second only to her happiness for him. She was so glad he'd seen the same thing in himself that she'd long known about him. He was a strong, honorable man with a huge, generous heart.

That he wanted to share it with her, and with Matthew, humbled her.

"I know you're going to love him and he's going to love you. You'll find your way together. I can't wait for you two to meet." She trailed her fingers over his lips, happy tears pricking her eyes. "And nothing would make me happier than to have you in my life. You're already in my heart."

He swept her off her seat and into his lap before she'd even seen him moving. Settled on his broad, splayed thighs, she wrapped her arms around his neck as his lips met hers.

He kissed her breathless, his heart beating a fast, erratic rhythm where her breasts pressed against his chest. That simple sign of emotion, of how much this moment meant to him, sent an added thrill through her.

When he edged back, his forehead tipped close, his sandalwood scent bringing back sensual memories.

"I've wanted to kiss you every second since I walked through that door." His lips trailed along her temple, then down her cheekbone. "I can't believe you're wearing the camisole that has haunted my every daydream since you picked up that video call."

Pleasure curled through her as it sank home that this incredible man loved her. That she had his heart as much as he had hers. That they would build a future together with Mattie.

"It seems fortuitous that you arrived at bedtime." The need to be with him, to wrap herself around him and feel how very real their future could be together, was a sudden imperative. "And as much as I really like you in a tuxedo, you're probably overdressed."

She felt his body react to that, and everything feminine inside her fluttered. He was already peeling away the cardigan from her shoulders.

"You like the tux?" His palm slipped under the strap of her camisole, skimming it aside. His voice was low and full of promise. "You'd be surprised how good I can make you feel while still wearing it."

Her mouth went dry. The fringe benefits from loving this man were going to be incredible. A sudden heat wave made her squirm in his lap, a move that had him bolting out of the chair with her in his arms.

"Your clothes have to go, however," he growled in her ear as he carried her through the living room to her bedroom. "That's a given."

He stole her breath as he settled her on her bed, his palms already tugging her pajama pants down her hips. His words continued to huff against her ear, a seduction that only heightened the way he touched her. "I might have you unfasten my cuffs, though. I'm going to need my hands for this."

A lightning bolt of sensation darted right though her, her only response a breathy moan as he kissed his way down her body. "I promise you, when I'm done, you'll be sure it's no dream."

And he was as good as his word, because he absolutely made her a believer.

Epilogue

Six months later

Squinting into the sunlight streaming through the tall pine trees along the edge of Gage's yard during a summer barbecue, Desmond tried to catch sight of Matthew on horseback with Marcus Salazar. Contentment rolled through him in waves. Life was good for him and Nicole and Matthew. And having his friends here for vacation only added to the fullness of his life.

Gage and Elena had decided to spend the summer at Mesa Falls after their honeymoon and ended up talking all the other owners and their significant others into doing the same. For the last two weeks, even Alonzo Salazar's sons had joined them, Marcus and Devon both accepting Weston's idea that they make it an annual trip with their families.

Now, Gage was in his element, grilling steaks near his pool while everyone else watched Jonah's baby daughter, Katja, take a few wobbly steps. The kid was adorable, and seeing Jonah as a dad gave Desmond more hope for his own parenting skills. Matthew had given him some confidence by making it easy on him the first time he'd met him, effectively interviewing Desmond for hours about his life, his job, his intentions toward Nicole, and all that had been before Matthew asked a single question about his biological father. The meeting had been scarier than the toughest job interview of his life, but he must have done okay, because Matthew had shaken his hand and welcomed him to the family before walking away to play video games.

Desmond couldn't love the kid more. Not just because he was Zach's son, but because he was an amazing individual, uniquely special in his own way.

He'd been even more grateful earlier in the summer when Matthew had agreed to Desmond's proposal—laid out in businesslike terms, because Matthew preferred to have all the facts—to adopt him once he married Nicole. But the thoughtful genius with dark eyes who shared more in common with Zach the more Desmond got to know him, had only further cemented their excellent bond that day by suggesting they make that date as soon as possible.

Nicole had married him in front of a judge two days later, making one of Desmond's biggest dreams come true. He'd been able to give Matthew his name and all the legal standing that brought with it right afterward, fulfilling a debt to his dead friend that had only added to the deepest sense of peace he'd ever known.

Although not being able to see Matthew through the trees right now was unsettling that peace a little. Marcus Salazar was an excellent rider, and he'd formed a tie with Matthew over their mutual interest in horses, so Desmond had figured it was okay to let them ride together. But they'd been gone half an hour.

"He's fine. You should come join us by the pool." Nicole's voice beside him soothed his worry almost as much as the warm press of her body, her thin summer dress printed with pretty flowers making his hands itch to peel it off her.

He'd never get used to the way she could ease him and stir him up at the same time. He hugged her closer, grateful for the feel of her curves and still not believing he got to call her his wife.

"In a minute." He kissed the top of her head while he kept his eyes trained on the trees. "How did you know what I was thinking?"

She laughed, a light, musical sound that sent a little more of his worry packing. "You mean how do I know you're the most adorable father of any fourteen-year-old ever? Only because I get to enjoy watching it every day we're here. I never want this summer to end. Seeing Matthew happy has brought me so much joy."

"You think he's okay?" Logic told Desmond he didn't need to worry while his son was with Marcus. But figuring out how to parent with a kid half-grown wasn't easy. Nicole, however, was a natural.

He turned his attention to her, trusting her.

"Remember his first two-hour interview when he met you?" she reminded him, threading her fingers through his as they walked toward the pool deck. "I'll bet he has a lot of questions for Marcus, too."

"He's an incredible kid." Desmond stopped short before they reached the others, letting himself take in the sight of all his friends gathered in one place.

Weston and his fiancée, April, were in the pool, Weston hanging off the side of her float while she sipped a margarita and fed him grapes. Gage was playing air guitar to the rock song that filtered through his outdoor speakers, while Elena, Astrid and Chiara danced in the grass.

Miles and Jonah had just started a game of horseshoes. Devon Salazar and his wife, Regina, took over watching Jonah's daughter. They were seated on either side of her baby blanket while Marcus's wife, Lily, supervised from a chaise lounge. Lily was very pregnant and Regina only a little less so. The Salazar brothers seemed to have healed their old rift, their wives obviously fast friends.

"He is an incredible kid," Nicole mused from beside him. "And he's got a fairly incredible life."

Desmond pulled her fully into the circle of his arms so he could see her lovely face. He leaned in to kiss her when she spoke again.

"The only thing he's missing is a sibling," she said in his ear.

A year ago the idea would have sent him running. Now? It felt so right he only wanted her all to himself to get started.

"Be careful what you say to me in public, wife." He couldn't resist lifting her in his arms. "I might give you exactly what you ask for."

Her flushed face was the best possible answer. But he put her back on her feet before he forgot all about the barbecue.

"Tonight," he warned her, as he headed for the cooler. He'd need something cold to get through the next few hours.

After that, he had every intention of making more of their dreams come true.

* * * * *

Dynasties: Mesa Falls
Don't miss a single installment!

The Rebel
The Rival
Rule Breaker
Heartbreaker
The Rancher
The Heir

by USA TODAY *bestselling author*
Joanne Rock

*Available exclusively
from Harlequin Desire.*

COMING NEXT MONTH FROM

HARLEQUIN

DESIRE

Available March 9, 2021

#2791 AT THE RANCHER'S PLEASURE
Texas Cattleman's Club: Heir Apparent • by Joss Wood
Runaway groom Brett Harston was Royal's favorite topic until Sarabeth Edmonds returned. Banished years before by her ex-husband, she's determined to reclaim her life and reputation. But a spontaneous kiss meant to rile up town gossips unleashes a passionate romance neither can ignore...

#2792 CRAVING A REAL TEXAN
The Texas Tremaines • by Charlene Sands
Grieving CEO Cade Tremaine retreats to his family's cabin and finds gorgeous chef Harper Dawn. She's wary and hiding her identity after rejecting a televised proposal, but their spark is immediate. Will the Texan find a second chance at love, or will Harper's secret drive him away?

#2793 WAKING UP MARRIED
The Bourbon Brothers • by Reese Ryan
One passionate Vegas night finds bourbon executive Zora Abbott married to her friend Dallas Hamilton. To protect their reputations after their tipsy vows go viral, they agree to stay married for one year. But their fake marriage is realer and hotter than they could've imagined!

#2794 HOW TO LIVE WITH TEMPTATION
by Fiona Brand
Billionaire Tobias Hunt has always believed the beautiful Allegra Mallory was only after his money. Now, forced to live and work together, she claims a fake fiancé to prove she isn't interested. But with sparks flying, Tobias wants what he can no longer have...

#2795 AFTER HOURS ATTRACTION
404 Sound • by Kianna Alexander
After finding out his ex embezzled funds, recording COO Gage Woodson has sworn off workplace romance. But when he's stranded with his assistant, Ainsley Voss, on a business trip, their chemistry is too hot to ignore. Will they risk their working relationship for something more?

#2796 HIS PERFECT FAKE ENGAGEMENT
Men of Maddox Hill • by Shannon McKenna
When a scandal jeopardizes playboy CEO Drew Maddox's career, he proposes a fake engagement to his brilliant and philanthropic friend Jenna Sommers to revitalize his reputation and fund her efforts. But as passion takes over, can this bad boy reform his ways for her?

YOU CAN FIND MORE INFORMATION ON UPCOMING HARLEQUIN TITLES, FREE EXCERPTS AND MORE AT HARLEQUIN.COM.

HDCNM0221

SPECIAL EXCERPT FROM

DESIRE

When a scandal jeopardizes playboy CEO Drew Maddox's career, he proposes a fake engagement to his brilliant and philanthropic friend Jenna Sommers to revitalize his reputation and fund her efforts. But as passion takes over, can this bad boy reform his ways for her?

Read on for a sneak peek at
His Perfect Fake Engagement
by New York Times *bestselling author Shannon McKenna!*

Drew pulled her toward the big Mercedes SUV idling at the curb. "Here's your ride," he said. "We still on for tonight? I wouldn't blame you if you changed your mind. The paparazzi are a huge pain in the ass. Like a weather condition. Or a zombie horde."

"I'm still game," she said. "Let `em do their worst."

That got her a smile that touched off fireworks at every level of her consciousness.

For God's sake. Get a grip, girl.

"I'll pick you up for dinner at eight fifteen," he said. "Our reservation at Peccati di Gola is at eight forty-five."

"I'll be ready," she promised.

"Can I put my number into your phone, so you can text me your address?"

"Of course." She handed him her phone and waited as he tapped the number into it. He hit Call and waited for the ring.

"There," she said, taking her phone back. "You've got me now."

"Lucky me," he murmured. He glanced back at the photographers, still blocked by three security men at the door, still snapping photos. "You're no delicate flower, are you?"

"By no means," she assured him.

"I like that," he said. He'd already opened the car door for her, but as she was about to get inside, he pulled her swiftly back up again and covered her mouth with his.

His kiss was hotter than the last one. Deliberate, demanding. He pressed her closer, tasting her lips.

Oh. Wow. He tasted amazing. Like fire, like wind. Like sunlight on the ocean. She dug her fingers into the massive bulk of his shoulders, or tried to. He was so thick and solid. Her fingers slid helplessly over the fabric of his jacket. They could get no grip.

His lips parted hers. The tip of his tongue flicked against hers, coaxed her to open, to give herself up. To yield to him. His kiss promised infinite pleasure in return. It demanded surrender on a level so deep and primal, she responded instinctively.

She melted against him with a shudder of emotion that was absolutely unfaked.

Holy crap. Panic pierced her as she realized what was happening. He'd kissed her like he meant it, and she'd responded in the same way. As naturally as breathing.

She was so screwed.

Jenna pulled away, shaking. She felt like a mask had been pulled off. That he could see straight into the depths of her most private self.

And Drew helped her into the car and gave her a reassuring smile and a friendly wave as the car pulled away, like it was no big deal. As if he hadn't just tongue-kissed her passionately in front of a crowd of photographers and caused an inner earthquake.

Her lips were still glowing. They tingled from the contact.

She couldn't let her mind stray down this path. She was a means to an end.

It was Drew Maddox's nature to be seductive. He was probably that way with every woman he talked to. He probably couldn't help himself. Not even if he tried.

She had to keep that fact firmly in mind.

All. The. Time.

Don't miss what happens next in…
His Perfect Fake Engagement
by New York Times *bestselling author Shannon McKenna!*

Available March 2021 wherever
Harlequin Desire books and ebooks are sold.

Harlequin.com

Get 4 FREE REWARDS!

We'll send you 2 FREE Books plus 2 FREE Mystery Gifts.

Harlequin Desire® books transport you to the world of the American elite with juicy plot twists, delicious sensuality and intriguing scandal.

FREE Value Over $20